for

better,

for

worse

for

—

better,

—

for

—

worse

—

A GUIDE TO

Surviving ·Divorce

FOR PRETEENS

AND THEIR FAMILIES

BY

Janet Bode AND Stan Mack

Simon & Schuster Books for Young Readers

New York London Toronto Sydney Singapore

Simon & Schuster Books for Young Readers
An imprint of Simon & Schuster Children's Publishing Division
1230 Avenue of the Americas, New York, New York 10020

Book design by Heather Wood
The text for this book is set in Stempel Schneidler.
The illustrations are rendered in pen and ink.
Printed in the United States of America
2 4 6 8 10 9 7 5 3 1

Library of Congress Cataloging-in-Publication Data
Bode, Janet.
For better, for worse: a guide to surviving divorce for preteens and their families /
by Janet Bode ; illustrations by Stan Mack.
p. cm.
Includes bibliographical references.
Summary: Uses first-person accounts from young people to describe the effects of divorce
and remarriage and how to handle them. Includes a section for adults discussing how to
minimize both the short- and long-term impact of divorce.
ISBN 0-689-81945-5
1. Children of divorced parents—Juvenile literature. 2. Divorce—Juvenile literature.
3. Remarriage—Juvenile literature. [1. Divorce. 2. Remarriage.] I. Title.
HQ777.5.B625 2001   306.89—dc21   99-462105

FIRST
F
EDITION

This book is dedicated to these remarkable teachers
and their equally remarkable students:

Ed Markarian
Benjamin Franklin High School
Los Angeles, California

Joy McKay
Argo Community High School
Summit, Illinois

With Thanks

Read this page and you can begin to trace the map of my journey to research this book. The individuals listed below invited me into their lives, their meetings, their libraries, and their classrooms. Without them I could not have even started this project. More to the point, I could never have finished it. My appreciation and thanks also go to the young people who shared their stories, poetry, art, and insight. They are the true experts on the topic.

Jan Balin and Abigail Yasgar, Jewish Family Service, West Hills, California; Agnes Beck, Andrew Heiskell Library for the Blind and Physically Handicapped, New York, New York; Diana Blitz, Edmund Burke School, Washington, D.C.; Aimee Buckner, Brookwood Elementary School, Snellville, Georgia; Jean Brown and Elaine Stephenson, Saginaw Valley State University, University Center, Michigan; Cornelia Corson and Cary Normile, Spence School, New York, New York; Tina Dickinson, Utah Corrections Association, Cedar City, Utah; Phyllis Fisher and Arlene Weber Morales, New York Public Library Books for the Teen Age Program, Donnell Center of the New York Public Library, New York, New York; Marianne Gregory, Franklin High School, Los Angeles, California; Dixie Hewitt, San Saba High School, San Saba, Texas; Dagmar Jaunzems, Canton Free Library, Canton, New York; Linda Johnson, Sem Yeto High School, Fairfield, California; Jeff Katz, Central Public Library, Seattle, Washington; Esther McCrae, Paul Robeson High School, Brooklyn, New York; Sybil Oster and Janet Gelfand, Lawrence Middle School, Lawrence, New York; Craig Roney, Wayne State University, Detroit, Michigan; Ellen Rubin, Wallkill Senior High School, Wallkill, New York; Caryn Sipos, King County Library System, Seattle, Washington; Larry Williams, Washington Heights Public Library, Bronx, New York.

Back on my global homefront continual support made all the difference during my year of work. I owe my family and friends big time, starting with my special partner-editor-cartoonist, Stan Mack; my sisters, Carolyn and Barbara; my extended family, the Lutzes, Kenny Mack, Peter Mack, Kerri Mahoney, Stephanie Ripple, Mike Sexton; my family of friends, Linda Broessel, Phyllis Cadle, Wendy Caplan, Chas Carner, Lucy Cefalu, Val and Ron Chernow, Kay Franey, Harriet and Ted Gottfried, Carole Mayedo, Rosemarie and Marvin Mazor, Betty Medsger, San San Tin, Deborah Udin; the now widely dispersed Third Thursday Group, including Kathryn Kilgore and Jane O'Reilly; the Beth Israel Medical Center doctors and technical staff, especially Ellen Gold, M.D., and Karen DeVries, who help me in my ongoing fight to beat back my breast cancer recurrence; and my thoughtful, patient editor, David Gale.

Contents

for

better,

for

worse

Part One ☀

For Girls and Boys

Introduction ☁

Picture a group of sixth- and seventh-grade students. They're talking to me—a writer—about divorce and remarriage. I want to know what they think should be in a book on these topics. Ten-year-old Christopher says, "Write a book that lets you know you're not the only one going through all this."

Venitia, age twelve, wants more details: "Have advice about disappearing dads, parents' dating, being fair, stepparents, half brothers and sisters, that kind of thing." When Ben, eleven, says, "Find real kids to tell their stories about these problems," they agree, that's the right idea. But when Samantha, ten, adds, "Make the book so good you feel better after reading it," the room grows silent. All of them come from families touched by divorce.

They've heard, they tell me, that when divorce and remarriage collide with your life, you are scarred forever. They want to know if that means you are doomed to an unhappy future, or can you pick up life's pieces, put them together, and successfully move on?

"I'll find out the truth," I answer.

THE SEARCH

I decided to go in search of people with information and advice on how best to survive a divorce and even a parent's marriage or two to someone new. For over a year I talked to adult experts: from divorce lawyers and counselors to countless divorced moms and dads. They offered their own experiences, insights, and theories on what individuals can do to build a healthy future.

At the same time I listened to what preteens and teenagers, experts in their own way, had to say based on firsthand knowledge. I visited towns as small as San Saba, Texas, population 2,626, and cities so big a single school's population was larger than that. With a tape running, I heard what groups of eight to fifteen students had to share about their family stories.

Afterward groups of fifty to one hundred of their classmates met with me in the library to learn about this project. When I asked, "Will any of you volunteer to record your thoughts about divorce or remarriage in words or pictures?" nearly everyone set to work. Some told me they wrote regularly—they kept journals. This day they wrote for fifteen minutes.

At the end of the period they handed in the results,

pieces of paper that opened the windows into their private worlds. Together, the words and pictures began to reveal how those events had shaped and molded their generation.

Next I turned to teachers for more in-depth help. I sent them a list of ways their students could be involved in the research for my book. Teachers I knew recommended teachers they knew. I E-mailed my request to one such teacher, Ed Markarian at Benjamin Franklin High School in Los Angeles, California. He turned it into a class assignment. Although his students were juniors and seniors, often they had had years of experience coping with divorce's aftereffects.

They went home, alone with their thoughts, and spent hours creating related projects. In poetry, essays, art, and lists of what was bad and good about coming of age in split families, they revealed themselves and their hearts. Their hope, they said, was that younger readers would benefit from this unique view of what might lie ahead.

Joy McKay, a teacher at Argo Community High School in Summit, Illinois, had her students write to me about their lives. For some, divorce or remarriage was the focus. Another teacher, Aimee Buckner at Brookwood Elementary School in Snellville, Georgia, asked third and fourth graders if they would help with this book in progress. Many answered yes.

One boy even said his divorced parents had agreed he could talk to me, just the two of us, on the phone. Students from Michigan, New York, and Colorado, among other places, followed his lead. They let me into their lives through phone conversations that sometimes lasted hours.

Some of these extended looks became the real-life short stories in chapter 3.

FOURTEEN MONTHS LATER

After fourteen months of cross-country talking, taping, listening, surveying, and questioning, I had collected more than a thousand individual family divorce and remarriage accounts. I had opinions on the same topics, these written by preteens and teenagers being raised by the parents they'd had since birth. And I had pages of notes from personal interviews and writing sessions with the adult experts I'd met nationwide.

I read everything. Then I read everything again. I had to decide what to leave out, what to leave in, and how to arrange that information. In the following chapters you'll find out what these experts, young and old, had to say. Because this book couldn't include all their wisdom, I chose the most-representative voices.

WHAT'S INSIDE

Part one looks at divorce and remarriage through the eyes of preteens and teenagers. In chapter 1 you find an overview of why divorce and remarriage can make you feel so lousy, along with the voices of boys and girls discussing their personal experiences. Next comes a survey, chapter 2, a chance to see how your feelings and responses to these issues compare to those of your peers.

In chapter 3 you meet Sam and his sister, Erin; Michael Elbaz; Lauren; and three more students. These are their real-life stories, told either in cartoon strips or words alone.

They focus on the problems and solutions created by divorce and remarriage. Included in this chapter are sidebars featuring advice from still other students.

Talking about your problems is helpful, but so is drawing or writing about them. Chapter 4 is a selection of preteens' and teenagers' work I collected when visiting schools.

Chapter 5 turns the platform over to those growing up in intact families. They feel there's misunderstanding on both sides of this issue, those in split families and those in families like theirs. This is a chance to bridge that divide.

The last chapter of part one answers questions about your future, focusing on two seventeen-year-olds' advice on how to achieve happy endings. Their belief is that what worked for them could work for you.

Part two is aimed at the adults in your world and the professionals whose job it is to try to help split families glue themselves back together. Adults read about the struggles and successes of a divorced mom and a divorced dad. They learn where to turn in their communities to take advantage of such services as the school-based Banana Splits program; a Jewish Family Service program, "Moving On," for divorced families; and so on. There's also a list of related books and on-line assistance.

Again and again the children and adults remind you, you're not on a solitary journey trying to build a new life on the remains of your old one. You have plenty of company. The marriage vows say "for better, for worse." Today—for better, for worse—split families are everyday common.

Chapter 1

Divorce is messy. So is remarriage. One family ends and new ones grow. To make sense of these changes, many students say that what helps most is to talk about them—and then listen to advice from others in similar situations.

Talk about what troubles you and the emotions you feel. Listen to how your friends deal with them. Talk about your hopes for the future. Listen to others' dreams and see what might feel right for you.

The voices set off below come from one of the discussions held by middle school students helping with this book. They touch on different experiences and emotions that may sound so familiar it's as if you're overhearing your own life story.

Sometimes, though, these life-changing events happen when you're too little to remember. You never hear Mom and Dad's speech on why they're going separate ways, who will live where, and how often—if ever—you'll see the one saying, "Good-bye, I'm leaving."

You are now bigger. Though you may have no old memories, your family complications continue, and they're as painful as those experienced by kids whose parents have divorced or remarried as recently as today.

Alice,* age twelve:

My parents separated when I was three. What I remember was no more screaming. Now I'm older. Mom says my dad won't divorce her because he still loves her. He doesn't come see us. He doesn't support us. Strange, huh? I never want to get married.

Christopher, age ten:

When I was five, my parents separated. They said, "It's not that we don't like each other. We just don't love each other anymore." Then they looked at me and said, "So how do you feel?" To this day I don't know what they expected me to answer.

THE FAMILY SCRIPT

Get a sheet of paper and on it write *Divorce/Remarriage*. Now fill the blank page with words that describe how these events make you feel. Maybe you'll put down *hurt, mad, sad, confused, ignored*. All these are normal

---

*Because this information is personal, the names are made up starting with Alice. In the real-life stories in chapter 3, some details were changed for even more privacy. (Two adults in part two asked for the same changes. Sometimes, though, you'll see a first and last name. These students and their parents gave permission not to change anything, the name included.)

reactions. What you might not know is why. There are two connected reasons.

To understand one reason, you have to understand something you could call the family script. Think of your life as a continuously running TV show. All programs have a script, and each family member is cast in one particular role. In the beginning let's say there's a mom and a dad, then along you come and, a little later, a sister or a brother.

For the show to succeed, for the family to run smoothly, all the actors have to perform their assigned role. And you have to stick to the family script. Imagine, though, what happens when a key actor, your mom or dad, quits the program. The script's been tossed out and no one is sure how to perform a new part.

You might have had clues that this change would happen. Maybe there've been upsetting nighttime fights, a silent anger filled with tension, or one parent simply vanishing. During that time you pretended everything was fine. In reality, these events make everyone feel off balance.

Venitia, age twelve:

Just before my parents split up, my dad told my mom she bought too much food. He said, "Your mother should be starved to death." Then he dumped everything on the kitchen floor. Next he came with a U-Haul truck while she was at work. He emptied the house and broke all the mirrors to give her bad luck.

Ben, age eleven:

When it first happened to me, my parents said, "Who do you

want to live with?" I was small. I said, "Mom." Now that I'm older, Mom's always asking, "Do you want to go live with your dad?" I feel if I say yes, she'll be mad at me. I hate when parents put you on the spot that way.

EXPLOSIONS

Because each family script is like a TV show, the way you act often depends on the way the other family members act and how each of them plays his or her role. When a divorce explodes in the heart of your family, everybody is wounded. Some members—even a parent—hurt so much that they feel they're dying. Emotionally they shut down.

Some respond to the first explosion by setting off others. You scream at your mom, your sister, your best friend. You quit caring about school, you shoplift, you cut yourself on purpose. It doesn't matter how exactly you react, one thing is clear: Separation, parents moving out, parents dating, divorce, and remarriage change a family script forever.

Jessica, age twelve:

You can be obnoxious with your parents' dates. Or if you really want to test them, ask for an expensive present. If you get one, it means they like both your parent and you.

Ben, age eleven:

What I care about is my parents dating. My mom says, "If you don't like the person, I'll get rid of him." But that's not how things have worked out.

Alice, age twelve:

We moved from a house to an apartment. Through the walls I can hear my mom and her latest boyfriend having sex. I hate it.

With all these changes you cannot expect your family to be calm. Parents feel guilty. You feel ignored. You or a sibling tries to fill the space left by the now-missing member. An older brother might act like Dad. If the mom moves out, maybe a sister takes on that role. You hope to play those parts plus your regular one, something that's almost impossible.

What you *need* is a new balance. What you often *want* is to get back what you lost. No matter how good or how troubled your family has been, it's what you know. And what you know brings you a certain comfort.

DEATH OF A FAMILY

Here is the second reason why divorce and remarriage bring on an exhaustion of emotions: A divorce often feels like the death of a family. You go through the same emotions that come when any loved one dies. You feel shocked, numb. Even if you're not surprised, you can't believe it is happening.

You worry you caused this. If only you hadn't picked on your brother, if only you had cleaned your room, if only . . . You bargain with your parents. You'll be good, you promise. You haven't yet learned that the divorce is not your fault.

You decide your parents are changing their minds; they are not divorcing. This is called denial, and in some ways it can help. It gives you a chance to catch your breath, sort out your life, and begin to make sense of what's occurring around you.

You get depressed and tired. Too many emotions pull your energy down. For some of you, the separation goes on and on. For others, you feel like your life went from living with married parents to living with divorced parents and a zillion complications overnight.

There are as many variations as there are families. A parent leaves emotionally but is still in the neighborhood or even the house. A parent vanishes never to reappear. A parent is already in love with someone new. The fights diminish. The fights increase. The topics are old. The topics are new. Money. Custody. Transportation arrangements for your travel back and forth between two homes. Routines no longer exist. Life seems to have no order. The adults you've relied on seem to have turned into . . . ? You're not even sure.

Peter, age eleven:

My parents are talking divorce and I'm thinking, Is it something I did? What happens now? Who do I live with? Will we still live together or will we separate? So many questions with no answers.

Kynda, age eleven:

When I was four, my father left my mother, my one-year-old brother, and me. My mom was sad and depressed. She'd lie on her bed crying. She'd forget to make dinner and I didn't know why.

Samantha, age ten:

With my parents, my mom was cheating on my dad. She'd say she was going to the park to feed the ducks. This guy would be there. He'd bring his kids, too. Even when I didn't know exactly who he was, I did bad stuff to him; like when my mom did his laundry, I cut a hole in his sock.

Heather, age nine:

My parents said, "Because we love you so much, we have joint custody." Now I'm growing up with two keys around my neck, Mom's house and Dad's. When I go home to empty houses, I feel lonely, not loved.

PUBLIC RECOGNITION

You're just a kid.

Of course it's tough trying to make sense of all this. One of your parents or both want you to accept something you most often don't want to accept. One of them may be fighting the change as hard as you.

Acceptance of a divorce is like acceptance of a death. It is the final stage. But when a loved one dies, there's public recognition. There's a ceremony. Relatives and friends comfort you. You're suffering a loss. You are supposed to be upset and grieve. You're supposed to feel as if you've been run over by a truck.

Half the marriages in America end in divorce. Yet, when there is one—the death of a family—no one still quite knows what to say or how to act. No one knows to expect all these emotions. And the range of feelings doesn't come in exact time periods: You're in shock for a month, then you move on to bargaining, denial, and so on. To make matters tougher, all these stages can happen at once. No one tells you you're not crazy. Experiencing these emotions is normal.

Venitia, age twelve:

With my family, first the fights were about child support. Since my dad wished my mom were dead, he didn't want to give us any money. If we asked, he said, "That's all you guys want from me." Now my mom's remarried, and any money from Dad is out of the question.

Samantha, age ten:

My dad complains, but he still pays. What upsets me, though, is he won't develop a real relationship with me.

Jessica, age twelve:

I see my dad about once a year. I ask him to spend Christmas with me. He ignores it. I ask him to come watch my drill team competition. He tells me he can't because of Lent. He's not even religious.

Christopher, age ten:

My parents only talk because they have to, like if my dad forgets the child support. December, oops, he didn't send it. That starts the war. Are you gonna to pay? Nope. Boom!

Maybe during the divorce what you hear from your mom or dad is, "Don't worry. Soon everything will be back to normal." But the truth is your family has to create a new normal. From the old family a new one—or two—will be born. Just when you think your life has calmed down, a parent announces, "I'm getting married." Now you have a whole new cast of characters added to your original family script, which brings you back to the beginning.

SPLIT-REMARRIED-RECONSTITUTED-BLENDED-ACCORDION FAMILIES

Every day about 1,300 new stepfamilies form. Call them split families, remarried families, reconstituted families, blended families, even accordion families, expanding and contracting with his kids, her kids, and their kids.

No matter what the name, it's tricky being a member. Think of the characters from *South Park* combining with the characters from *Dawson's Creek*. What would these two family scripts have in common? They look at life through two different points of view. Mush them together and you have a ready-made stage on which battles can rage.

Once more, adults want you to accept a series of changes: share your life, share your room, share your privacy with a bunch of weirdo strangers. Are they crazy? You're way cool, and overnight Kenny, some freaky kid who drops dead every episode, is your stepbrother?

Or maybe they are kids you know from school. It doesn't mean you have anything more in common. In fact, you haven't liked them since you first met in second grade. And you're supposed to feel close to stepsiblings you didn't even choose?

Then another announcement—a new baby, your half sibling—and the complications increase. You may feel you have less and less importance in your parent's life. For some of you, too, this isn't the first time or possibly the last time that one or both of your parents will try to live happily ever after.

Zane, age twelve:

My father doesn't call often, and he puts my stepmother and stepsisters ahead of me. I feel he doesn't love me. I understand the emotional roller coaster, the wanting to be loved, the thoughts of suicide just to find a way to deal with problems. Somehow, when you are upset about a divorce, your everyday problems seem to be linked to it.

Kevin, age eleven:

My mom's married again. Sometimes I call him Dad. When I get mad at him, I call him by his first name.

David, age twelve:

Craig, my stepfather, handles the discipline. My mom stands by and watches. Moms let the stepdads take over the rules because they don't want to lose them and go through another divorce.

Ben, age eleven:

My stepmother plays favorites. My dad says it's because her kids don't come over a lot. When they do, she treats them special.

Kevin, age eleven:

My stepsister and I used to boss each other around. She thinks she's smarter because I'm younger. Now we get along better.

Venitia, age twelve:

Since my mom married Jason, I'm kind of scared of him. Every time I walk by he goes, "Here comes the pain in the . . ." My mom says, "Oh, he's kidding around."

Everything in your life is out of balance. One day your mom's the boss. The next day along comes this replacement, a stepparent. Or you were the youngest, the sweet baby. You were treated as if you were special. You liked your role. You didn't even think about it. Then suddenly there's a younger stepsibling and you're stuck in the middle. Changes upon changes can cause problems for everyone.

But, then again, they don't have to.

Dana, age twelve:

My second dad adopted me, so in a lot of ways that divorce was harder than the first. Now I'm twelve. My mom has been happily married for two years. I don't talk to my dad that adopted me anymore, but I wish I did. I'm fine, though, with the stepdad I have now, as long as my mom is happy.

Matt, age twelve:

A good thing about divorce is freedom. Not just for the parents, but also you. The two parents make two sets of rules. Some rules you agree with, most you don't. Usually in that situation you can pick favorites.

Another good thing is meeting new people. You meet your dad's new girlfriend and your mom's new boyfriend. The oddest times are accepting stepparents. Being the child, you will probably have little control over who your parents choose. So you might hate them or you might like them.

I think the nice part of having stepparents is all the new things they bring into your world. My parents are divorced. I don't think they should get back together. Mom is happy. Dad is happy. Nothing needs to be changed.

Ben, age eleven:

You can't just forget how divorce feels. You can't just forget how remarriage changes things. Your feelings build up inside. You should find a bunch of different ways to cope. Like, I showed up today for this book meeting. I talked about my problems. I'm glad I did. I feel better.

Chapter 2

The Survey: Filling in the Blanks

Some parents separate but never divorce. Some marry and divorce several times. Some never marry each other but have children together. Although no single survey can easily cover all combinations, the following questions deal with many of those situations. Young people age eight to fourteen who have experienced these life changes suggested what questions to include.

Then other students from places such as Fairfield, California; Washington, D.C.; and Lawrence, New York, completed the survey. If you'd like to compare your responses to theirs, answer these fourteen questions on a blank sheet of paper. To see how your peers responded, turn to page 23.

Other girls and boys had more to say than would fit in these blanks. They decided to write a sentence or two of their best advice on how to handle eleven typical problems. The difficulties range from what to do when a stepparent puts down your real parent to dividing up the holidays. Throughout chapter 3 you'll find their suggestions.

The Bode Survey on Divorce and Remarriage

1. Were you surprised when you learned that your parents were separating/divorcing? ___yes ___no

2. Once your parents separated, did you feel left in the dark about what was going on between them? ___yes ___no

3. Do you feel the separation/divorce was your fault? ___yes ___no

4. Have you ever had to choose which parent to live with? ___yes ___no

   If yes, which one did you choose? ___mother ___father

5. Do you still feel loved by both your parents? ___yes ___no

6. Since the separation/divorce, has your standard of living dropped—there used to be enough money and now there isn't? ___yes ___no

7. Do you feel like a Ping-Pong ball between your parents?
___yes ___no

8. When was the last time you saw the parent you don't live with? _____

   About how many times a year do you see him/her?_____

9. If you have a stepparent (or a live-in adult), does that person try to replace your real parent? ___yes ___no

10. If your stepparent (or live-in adult) and your real parent fight, do they make you feel it's your fault? ___yes ___no

11. Do you have any stepsiblings? ___yes ___no

    Half siblings? ___yes ___no

    Do you feel you are favored over them? ___yes ___no

12. As a result of the separation/divorce do you feel (check any that describe you): ___sad ___angry ___lonely ___troubled ___relieved ___happy ___worried about your future ___you do better in school ___you do worse in school ___no change in school ___changes in your friendships ___in need of therapy ___more responsible ___more grown-up

    Write in feelings not listed: _____

13. Do you hope that your parents will get back together?
    ___yes ___no

14. Do you understand why your parents felt it was necessary
    to separate/divorce? ___yes ___no

Results of the Bode Survey on Divorce and Remarriage

Seventy-five students age eight to eighteen volunteered to complete this survey. They attended a range of schools— public and private; urban, suburban, and rural. Because some left questions blank and some were too young to answer when the divorce took place, the responses won't always total seventy-five.

1. Were you surprised when you learned that your parents were separating/divorcing? 25 yes / 33 no

2. Once your parents separated, did you feel left in the dark about what was going on between them? 19 yes / 39 no

3. Do you feel the separation/divorce was your fault? 9 yes / 62 no

4. Have you ever had to choose which parent to live with? 29 yes / 41 no

   If yes, which one did you choose? 23 mother / 6 father

5. Do you still feel loved by both your parents? 54 yes / 20 no

6. Since the separation/divorce, has your standard of living dropped—there used to be enough money and now there isn't? 16 yes / 47 no

7. Do you feel like a Ping-Pong ball between your parents? 30 yes / 44 no

8. When was the last time you saw the parent you don't live with?
   Days ago: 39
   Months ago: 10
   One to five years ago: 7
   More than five years ago: 9
   Never in your memory: 2

   About how many times a year do you see him/her?
   Zero to three times: 22
   Four to twelve times: 6
   Twelve to fifty times: 18
   More than fifty times: 21

9. If you have a stepparent (or a live-in adult), does that person try to replace your real parent? 25 yes / 17 no

10. If your stepparent (or live-in adult) and your real parent fight, do they make you feel it's your fault? 15 yes / 36 no

11. Do you have any stepsiblings? 23 yes / 34 no

Half siblings? 29 yes / 24 no

Do you feel you are favored over them? 7 yes / 25 no

12. As a result of the separation/divorce, do you feel (check
    any that describe you): 33 sad / 28 angry / 16 lonely
    25 troubled / 16 relieved / 12 happy / 15 worried about
    your future / 5 you do better in school / 13 you do worse
    in school / 25 no change in school / 13 changes in your
    friendships / 11 in need of therapy / 19 more responsible /
    32 more grown-up

    Write in feelings not listed:
    I feel unloved and unwanted.
    I feel the same, no change.
    I'm concerned that my mom will be alone.
    I live in a foster home. I wish my parents were around,
        but they aren't. I haven't seen my mom in seven and a
        half months, my dad in three years.
    The divorce makes me feel like I am a toy.
    I feel we're better off without my dad.
    It's calmer in my house now.
    It makes me feel awful. My brother treats my mom bad
        and my dad good.

13. Do you hope that your parents will get back together?
    14 yes / 53 no

14. Do you understand why your parents felt it was necessary
    to separate/divorce? 51 yes / 16 no

Chapter 3

. . . Along with Advice from Other Kids and Therapists

Around the country elementary and middle schools have organized programs (see part two, page 131) to help you sort out your life's pieces and begin to reassemble them. With adult guidance you and other classmates going through the same things meet regularly to talk about your problems.

What's said in that room stays there. Everything is confidential. And even when they can't find all the answers, those who participate say in the end they feel better. It often hurts to keep your pain inside. It often hurts less to let the pain out.

If you aren't sure whether your school has such a program, ask a counselor, teacher, librarian, or assistant principal. One or all of those people will know.

You may not want to talk about problems in front of kids you know in school. You feel shy, embarrassed, uncomfortable, or all those combined. Or you feel okay being part of this kind of group, but you want more. You know that talking about what's in your heart is important, but you want to do it on your own schedule: when it hurts the most, when you're most confused, when you feel you're going to explode.

And you know this isn't just a one-time conversation. There's too much to say for a single talk. Plus, what troubles you today may not cause the most pain tomorrow.

Preteens and teenagers nationwide say it's best to talk to whoever you think will bring you comfort. You should look for a good and trusted listener. You're the expert in deciding who that person should be, and it can be more than one individual.

Maybe right now your mom's the best listener. Maybe later it's your dad, or even later, both of them. You could also turn to a favorite aunt, your grandfather, your best friend's mother, the lady next door who's been in your life forever, the librarian who always makes time for you, the teacher who likes you, the minister who runs your Sunday school—or a therapist.

PROBLEMS AND SOLUTIONS

In this chapter, seven real kids share their stories. Following each one, three New York City family therapists—Clio Garland, Ann Jackler, and Andrea Osnow—tell you what problems they see and what might be done to solve them.

Maybe you hear parts of what you're experiencing echoed in the words spoken by these girls and boys. And just maybe what the therapists have to say feels right to you.

Garland, Jackler, and Osnow have practices where they specialize in the problems of families. They are friends, too. Before talking about Sam and his sister, Erin; Lauren; and the rest, they read the students' accounts. Then they sat around a table discussing each story. Often one would present an idea and another would add more details, finishing the thought, just the way you might talk with a good friend. Their hope is that the information they offer helps you figure out what's what in your own situation.

Throughout this chapter you'll come across "Kid Problem, Kid Solutions" sidebars. Children from families living with divorce and remarriage suggested eleven key problems with which they have wrestled. Other boys and girls in the same situation came up with advice and solutions they said they had used successfully. When you read them, you'll see that the students don't always agree with one another, and none of the advice comes with a guarantee. You will have to decide for yourself which of the suggestions are totally impractical, which are practical, and which might help in your situation. If nothing else, you can pick and choose a starting point to find your own answers.

I'M GOING TO USE A BAD WORD. THREE <u>DANG</u> YEARS AGO, WHEN I WAS SEVEN YEARS OLD AND MY SISTER, ERIN, WAS FOUR, OUR PARENTS GOT DIVORCED.

WHEN THEY FOUGHT, ME AND ERIN HID IN OUR ROOMS. I'D PUT MY HEAD UNDER MY PILLOW.

WHEN MY PARENTS FOUGHT, MY FINGERS WOULD GET TIGHT. GOING FISHING AND PLAYING VIDEO GAMES HELPED LOOSEN THEM.

SOME PEOPLE GET DIVORCED BECAUSE THEY HIT EACH OTHER. OR THE MAN MAKES HIS WIFE CLEAN THE DISHES ALL THE TIME.

Divorce hurts a lot at first. Children have all sorts of angry, sad, and lonely feelings. It's important to share them with each parent. Brothers and sisters can help one another, too. You can talk about feelings, ask questions, and comfort each other. No one else knows how hard the family situation is except those going through it with you.

OKAY FIGHTS

Sam and Erin have a wonderful, totally normal brother-sister relationship. Together they weather the storms around them. Some kids come to believe that problems should never be worked out through fights. Well, fighting is a natural part of life. There are always going to be differences. You have to be able to argue about them. If you can't, you can't be really close to someone. The goal is to manage the problems so you feel things are resolved and you can move on. You discover anger doesn't mean you don't love each other anymore.

In some families the parents never fight. They don't even know how to bring up problems in order to try to find solutions. Instead maybe one of the parents has an affair or becomes a workaholic. This keeps the marriage going for a while. Then one day they announce, "We're getting a divorce and Dad's moving out." This is called the silent divorce. It is really confusing for children.

FAIRNESS

Fairness is interesting to think about. Kids always evaluate and yardstick who got more. Does it mean giving the same present to each person? Does each person get the same amount of attention? When there's a divorce, worries about being fair to each child and each parent can increase. No one wants to lose out.

Sam worries about fairness. Still, you can see that as he got used to his new schedules and living situations he felt better. It's great when parents work together to take care of their children even though they live in separate homes. Yes, everyone has a crazy schedule, but it means Sam and Erin see both parents almost daily. Their parents deserve a lot of credit. And good for Sam for realizing that getting through the emotions of divorce takes time. It doesn't happen overnight.

KID PROBLEM, KID SOLUTIONS

If I'm asked, how do I decide which parent to live with?

☞ Pick whichever one you think can give you the better life. It doesn't mean you love the other one less.

☞ Think hard about what place you'd feel the safest and most comfortable.

☞ Look at all the positives and negatives of both, and follow your heart to where you'll be the happiest.

☞ Go with the one headed in the right direction.

☞ Think about this: How often will you see the parent you are not with? Who are you closer to? Who can take better care of you without getting stressed?

☞ You shouldn't have to choose. I've lived with both and learn different things at each place. It's made me stronger.

MICHAEL ELBAZ'S STORY, AGE NINE

Brookwood Elementary School, Snellville, Georgia

Here's a poem I just felt like writing. I call it "Divorce."

First yelling
    then hollering
        then shouting
            then screaming
then not known until I
    have to get a
drink of water at midnight.

    No more snoring noises
just the Channel Two Action News
    then
        I peer outside
one van
        no jeep.

        I go into the bathroom
no black toothpaste tube or
    toothbrush.
    No drip
        drip
            drip noises coming
from the sink.

    I wake up Sara. As I
show her all the things that are missing
    she screams in horror as she stares

at the fish tank.
She is right—
    there is no fish.

    We sob ourselves
    to sleep that night.

In the morning
I see two figures on the edge
    of my bed.
I recognize them.
    They are my mom
    and my dad with very harsh
faces on.
They tell me
    that they are finally

DIVORCED!

Exact Day

    I remember the exact day my dad moved out. That morning I rode the school bus with my sister Sara, the way I always do. (I have a baby sister, Rebecca, too.)

    After lunch I went from person to person and told my entire class what had happened. "My parents got a divorce," I said. I was upset. Kids like Logan and Eric said they were kind of surprised, but I wasn't alone. There were other kids right in the room with that experience.

    I wished it was a bad dream. If I begged my parents, maybe they'd change their minds.

Love Cards

On Valentine's Day the teacher said we had to make love cards for our parents. I made two of them, one for my mom and one for my dad. First I put, like, double *E*s facing the opposite way. In the clear spots between the two lines top and bottom, I made frames for the pictures I was going to draw.

Inside one of the frames the dad has a suitcase. He walks out the door and says to the mom, "Let's not meet again." She goes, "Oh, swell," and they both drop their rings on the ground.

Then I drew the dad holding a dead flower and the mom walking away. In the other card I did the opposite—the mom is holding the dead flower and the dad is walking away.

In the next picture the dad is calling us on the phone. He's going to tell my sister Sara he forgot her shoes. I'm talking to him and say, "Hey, Dad, do you want to talk to Mom?" I hear from him a huge, "NO!" On the mom card she's the one to yell, "NO!" She doesn't want to talk to Dad.

In the last picture on both cards there's a sign with the word DIVORCE on it. The letter *V* is a heart broken in half. All around the word are frowning faces, especially Mom's and Dad's.

I didn't have enough time to color the cards. Still, drawing and writing them helped me feel better. When I showed them to my friends, they said, "That's sad."

At home after school my parents were both there having an argument. My dad was saying to my mom, "If I had a girlfriend, she'd be way nicer than you." I gave them the cards and said, "I'm going upstairs to play Nintendo." Once

I got to the top of the stairs, I tried to peek to see their reaction. They were frowning, just like on my cards.

Mom hung hers on the refrigerator, until the baby, Rebecca, tried to eat the card and it ended up in the trash can. When I went to Dad's house, he had hung his on the refrigerator, too, but under something.

KID PROBLEM, KID SOLUTIONS

How do I handle times of the year – like holidays – when both parents want me to be with them?

- I've tried these ways: divide the holidays equally, switch years, or spend half the day with each one.
- It's too hard. Let your parents decide.
- Go with one parent one holiday, the other parent the next holiday. Visit the one you don't live with.
- Hang out with your friends and try to forget it's a holiday.
- My dad gets me every Jewish holiday. My mom gets me on the other ones. Try something like that.
- On Christmas spend the night at your dad's house, and in the morning, after you open all his presents, go to your mom's house and open presents there.

Dad and Mom

I love my dad and my mom. Right now my dad lives twenty minutes from here with my granddad. When I stay there, I sleep in the room with the computer and a bird in a cage. Its name is Big Bird. I know kids over there, but they're usually not outside screaming and playing.

My dad is fun. He lets Sara and me sleep in his room late into the morning. He takes us to the park to fly kites and to run around like chickens with our heads cut off. When we go anyplace, Sara usually wants to sit in the front of the Jeep next to him. I want to sit there, too, so we fight. Now even Rebecca, the baby, has started saying, "My turn."

I admit it, sometimes I boss Sara around. But I know how to give Rebecca a bath. Dad has to deal with three children at once. Luckily Granddad helps. He's from Israel. He speaks lots of languages. My dad's from Morocco. He's Jewish.

My mom's not. She's from here, Georgia. At my mom's we live in a yellow house with six televisions. I have a big room of my own filled with science things. When I do something wrong, the science kit fizzes or blows up. I used to have a TV and a VCR in my room, but Nintendo kept me up all night. I read a lot, too.

My mom's serious but really nice. She doesn't snore at night like my dad does. She bought me two Nintendo systems and sold my old one even though it was still entertaining. She's stricter than my dad. Maybe that's because she's a judge. There's another boy at school whose mom is a lawyer, and he says she's strict, too.

My parents compete over me.

My Secrets

My mom and dad had the divorce almost a year ago. By now it's kind of fine with Sara and me. It feels long since it happened. Rebecca's only two. She doesn't know what's what.

For me three things have helped the most: writing, Nintendo, and especially punching bags. I have a bag here and one at my dad's to help me let out the mad feelings. My mom filled this one with old, raggy carpet. That's why it feels weird. But I hit it—*POW!*—anyway, the same as I do at my dad's. I tell myself—*POW!*—"Don't worry about the divorce. Put it out of your mind." That's my secret on how to get through this.

WHAT THE THERAPISTS SAY

Michael has a gift. He uses his amazing creativity to express himself. Any outlet you can come up with, from a punching bag to talking, can help you get through a divorce. They are all appropriate.

He also seems to know the importance of turning to a sister or brother to share the sorrow. Too often siblings stop talking. This makes it harder.

Friends

Michael has the ability, too, to tell his friends, and they are there for him. He knows how to reach out to people, another real talent. He takes it a step further. He makes those powerful Valentine cards, where he shows how he sees the divorce. His friends look at them and have a clear understanding of what Michael's going through.

There's a valuable message for everyone in his cards. Children and parents need to know that with separation and divorce, the family as you knew it has died. Just like when there's the death of a loved one, you have to grieve for what was lost. You may need to mark the occasion in some real way, like the way a funeral marks a death. The rest of the message is that you'll get over your pain. A new family will be born. You'll figure it out as time goes by.

Through Michael you learn that divorce itself does not have to cause problems. People tend to think that the effects of divorce on children can be terrible and last a lifetime. People grow up and say, "I'm the child of divorce. I can't fall in love. I can't have a long-term relationship."

Parent

How the parents deal with the divorce determines whether their children will have problems that never go away or whether they can move on. Michael's parents seem to be working together for the good of their kids. There seems to be a lot of strength in the family. Yes, it's unfortunate that divorce has to happen; it can frequently be a traumatic event. But the way the family manages it is what matters most in the long run.

·ᐁ·

KID PROBLEM, KID SOLUTIONS

How do I put up with feuding parents?

☞ Since you can't stop their fights, go to your bedroom, lock the door, open the window, and see how far you can hit some golf balls . . . or put on your favorite song and play it really loud . . . or say to yourself over and over, "It's boring to listen to parents argue."

☞ Do something wrong so they'll have to work together to help you.

☞ If it gets really bad, go stay at a friend's house for a while.

- Tell them, "I'm the kid. I didn't get this divorce. Don't make me carry messages back and forth. It isn't fair to put me in the middle!"
- Spend time alone with one parent without the other around.
- Tell the one you trust more and see if he or she can help stop the fighting.
- Stay out of the way and let them fight. You can't control it.
- Ask for advice from an adult who won't take sides.

JOSEPH'S STORY, AGE SEVEN

The lady is giving a Valentine card to her husband, telling him that she loves him with all her heart.

Her husband says, "Liar," takes the card, rips it up, and throws it in her face. When he even spanks the kid and tells him to move, the lady starts crying.

Her husband turns around and walks away. Through her tears she begs, "Don't leave." "Shut up," he says, and then pushes his crying child. Since that day, the lady and her husband have never seen each other. They got a divorce and now the poor kid has no father.

WHAT THE THERAPISTS SAY

For parents like this dad it's easier to leave a family when they are angry. Instead of telling the truth—he doesn't want to be married anymore or he no longer loves her—he gets mad at both his wife and their child.

This little boy—and those of you like him—should know the argument and the divorce have nothing to do with you. And you can't do anything to change what's happened. It's hard to understand why a dad wouldn't want to visit his child or stay in touch, but the reality is it happens.

Better Off Without Me

Some adults are irresponsible because the pain is great. Their disappearance has nothing to do with how lovable you—the child—are. They do care, but they don't have another way to deal with their guilt except to go away.

After a while they say to themselves, "Well, it's been three . . . four . . . five years. I don't want to interrupt my kid's life. He's better off without me."

Whatever happens, you can't divorce that father-son/father-daughter relationship. That man will always be your dad. He's just not there for you. Some family member, maybe your mom or your grandparent, can help you contact him so one day you can have a relationship.

If that's not possible, they could find a photo of your father. It doesn't have to be a recent one. It can be from back when your dad was growing up, to show that the person who left was once a boy, too.

You could also write your dad a letter with questions you have. You could tell your father about yourself. Even if you never send the letter, a lot of young people say that just writing something like this helps you feel better. You come to see that your dad doesn't understand that what he did hurts.

Fantasy

If you do try to find your father, you may have this fantasy: You knock on a door, and Dad opens it and covers you with hugs and kisses. In real life that parent may not want to see you. Then you not only feel like a failure, you feel like you did something wrong. You need to be prepared before you go.

Everything we've said about a disappearing dad is just as true if the mom is the one to vanish.

I was born in Montana, my mom and dad's first child. I think they were married two years. One day, though, my dad just up and vanished. My only memory of him is when I was, maybe, four. Mom dropped me off at my grammy's house, stayed a couple minutes, and left.

Grammy pointed across the room and said, "Lauren, why don't you go over and say hi to that fellow." It was my dad, her son. I guess he recognized me—but I don't think he would have been there if he'd known I was coming. I'd heard so many bad stories. He probably thought I hated him.

Another time at Grammy's house I noticed a new picture of my dad. He was with this woman—his wife—and their daughter. I started to wonder, Would my sister from him like me? What about his wife? I wanted to meet him again, but not enough to search for him.

My Stepdad, Another Story

I was five when I got my stepdad, Zach. He came to help our neighbors move out of their apartment. I'd never seen him before, but he knew my mom. Suddenly, like— boom—he was in my life.

They married, and my mom had two more children, Nell and Harry, two years apart. Some kids get jealous. I wasn't. I was always wanting to play with them, especially outdoors, except in the spring. I have bad allergies. Then we'd play dress-up inside.

Anyway, from the beginning Nell, Harry, and I got along. We've had our fights, but no more than normal. The same with my stepdad's son, Zach Junior. He was one of those every-other-weekend kids. We both have blond hair and blue eyes. People confused us for brother and sister. My mom's more like a big sister. She knows where I'm coming from. I love her.

How I feel about my stepdad is another story. I don't think he ever liked me. I took my mom's attention away from him. He wanted it all. See, he was adopted. His parents were mean to him.

Gradually he started being mean, not to Nell or Harry, but to me. Little by little it got worse. I figured he'd picked just one of us to be mean to, and I was the one. When he hit me, he said, "I'm beating you because that's all I knew." Once we were out back and my sister fell. He thought I'd thrown her down. He picked me up by my hair and threw me halfway across the yard. It was scary.

My mom saw it. She told him, "You ever do that again, we're gone." He stopped, but he'd still do what you might call odd things. He told me stuff he shouldn't have, like that he did drugs, and he told me things about a girl at school who didn't like me. He said her parents only got married because the mom was pregnant.

Then he said, "Lauren, you're nothing special either. Your parents married for the same reason. They didn't love each other."

I started crying. When I asked my mom, she said, "That's not true." I kept some other things he did secret from my mom. I was scared if I told her, he'd find out. Then I'd really be in trouble. Anyway, I told my best friend, Jennifer. Jennifer told her mom, and her mom told mine. Everything happened—and nothing.

What should I do if my dad/mom promises to come over but doesn't show up?

☞ It's not you. They're hurting deep inside and have to figure out their life. It's not fair, but it doesn't mean you're forgotten.

☞ Tell them you don't like it when they break promises. You love and miss them.

☞ There's nothing you can do, so try not to think about it. Do it back to them and then say, "See how it feels? Can we talk about it?"

☞ Ask them why and then try to be understanding.

☞ Try to ignore them, call a friend or just comfort yourself.

☞ Don't feel discouraged. Keep living your life. You'll see that parent again sometime.

☞ Act like you're doing all right without them.

☞ Tell them that you know it's probably hard for them, but it's twice as hard for you.

☞ Tell them you feel hurt that you can't trust them to show up and you'd like to trust them.

A Confusing Time

My stepdad worked, but usually he was home in the afternoon. I'd come home from school with homework to do. He'd start yelling, "Clean the kitchen, Lauren!" Mom told him to do it, and he was trying to pass it off on me. He'd go crazy, so I'd clean. Then Mom would come home, see the kitchen, and praise him.

One night at the dinner table Harry was going around the room saying what everybody did. He said, "Mom works at an office with a computer. Lauren and us go to school. And Daddy's job is to lie on the couch and sleep."

Since he owned his own business, he only worked on the days he wanted. Most days he didn't want to work. He didn't get much money. If it weren't for my nana and my poppy, my mom's parents, we might not have survived.

A lot of times during those years my mom would say, "This is it. I won't take it anymore. Lauren, we're leaving." But we never did—until the day she called Nana to come from Colorado to pick us up. In the middle of packing, my stepdad came home. He tried to talk us out of leaving, but it didn't work. We were tired of his excuses.

Three days later my grandmother pulled up in front of school. I wanted to say good-bye to Jennifer. We never fought the whole four years I knew her. We just had fun together. I got her out of class. "We're leaving this minute," I told her, and then we hugged for a long time. I was ten years old. It was hard to walk away from one life and into another.

My nana, my mom, Nell, Harry, and I hit the road in a great big van packed with everything in the world we owned.

Any Questions

We moved in with my grandparents one week before Christmas. We were cramped all together. Poppy used a bedroom for an office. The three kids were in another room, and Mom was on the couch.

I missed my friends. I was scared of going to a new school. What if no one liked me? That first day, midyear in fifth grade, I walked through the doors. I remember the school smelled like good food and erasers. The counselor met me in the office and took me to my classroom. I'd never had a locker before, and she showed me how to use one. I had a nice teacher, too. Miss Dearman. She retired last year. She was winding down and wasn't that strict.

I enjoyed that school more than any I've gone to. I began to learn who was who. I started in the popular crowd, but I'm not thin and didn't make it. So I moved down. That was okay. When I was in sixth grade, I was in the gifted and talented program. Bridget was my study buddy. Then I met Kaysie, Joanne, and Betsy. I liked them a lot.

Edge of the Planet

To this day, two years after we left him, my stepdad calls. He upsets everyone. He's all sweet and apologizes for not calling before. He tries to get back with my mom. When that doesn't work, he yells, "There's a law that says I can take the kids from you." Then it quiets down for a month or two until it starts over.

He says he's coming to see us. He never does. I don't have to see him. But I won't say I want him to fall off the edge of the planet and disappear. We lived together for seven years. I can't just forget him. Nell and Harry miss him. They think he doesn't love them. My mom and I make up some story to make them feel better.

I'm twelve now. We just moved into a two-bedroom, two-bathroom apartment. It's not nasty or full of cockroaches. There are people my age. It's good but hard to be here. We were so used to being around Nana and Poppy. "It's for the best," my mom says.

I'm going into seventh grade and starting another school. I'm nervous. You know how it is. You have to learn who you can hang out with and who you can't. I love drama club and speech competitions. I hope I can do that and make friends.

Pay More Attention

As I grow up I try not to think too far ahead—more day by day. In a way I'm glad that I've gone through all this, so maybe these experiences won't have to happen to me. I'm more cautious than I would have been. I pay more attention to the small things that can turn into big problems. And I tell myself that everything in my life is getting better.

WHAT THE THERAPISTS SAY

Lauren is remarkable. Even though she's had trouble in her life, she still studies, has good friends, and is nice to her sister and brother. She's smart, optimistic, and knows herself. Those are good gifts to have.

She evaluates things. She doesn't jump to judgments. It's impressive how she tries to sort out why her stepdad was mean to her. With friends and in families someone may be turned into the scapegoat, the one picked on. She hasn't figured out yet it has nothing to do with her.

And although she's scared to tell her mom about her stepdad's behavior, she knows to turn to someone. For Lauren it's her best friend, but adults, like a teacher or counselor, can help, too. Some children worry they'll upset Mom if they tell her certain things. It's okay to upset your mother. She needs to know and to protect you. If you're sure she's the wrong person, find adults you trust and tell them. You need to talk, especially when you're treated cruelly.

Leaving even bad situations can be hard. Lauren knows she's going to miss her friends and her life at that school. She may also discover it's not unusual to still feel connected to her stepdad. She probably hopes he'll change. Meanwhile, she focuses on normal issues, like fitting in at a new school.

As with Lauren, it's common in divorced families for the child of the first marriage to be close to the mother. If Lauren is too responsible for taking care of the kids from the second marriage, it can become a problem.

Lauren's a survivor. She comes to terms with a parent who has disappeared from her life. She knows the benefit of having strong ties with grandparents. For all her family tension and moves, she is a warm, trusting human being.

-ᗛ-

KID PROBLEM, KID SOLUTIONS

What if my dad/mom is so busy with a new life that I feel forgotten?

☞ Tell them that even though their life is changing, you're as much a part of it as before.

- Try to include yourself in their new life or focus on the things in your life that make you happy.
- Tell them how much you miss those moments when you were together.
- Maybe it makes you feel sad and angry, but after a while you'll get used to not seeing them.
- Find times to call them, or if you have a computer, send them E-mail.
- Tell them that you're still their kid and they have an obligation to keep you in their life.
- Some parents are workaholics and nothing changes them.

KID PROBLEM, KID SOLUTIONS

What should I do if my dad's girlfriend/mom's boyfriend (or new spouse) is always yelling at me for no good reason?

- Understand that it is not okay. You don't have to take it. Talk to an adult you trust about what he or she thinks you should do.
- Bite your tongue. Nothing they say can really do anything to you.
- Ask your biological parent or that person why they're doing that.
- Sometimes nothing you say or do is good enough for them. They'll yell about the one thing you miss. You just have to learn to live with it until you're older and out of the house.
- Try to let it go in one ear and out the other. If that doesn't work, go outside and play, punch a wall as long as it's not brick, slam the door of your room, and beat up a pillow.
- Don't run away. Talk about it.

How do I deal with my stepparent treating his/her kids better than me?

☞ They might not be used to having new kids, so they're just ignorant and don't know how to act. It's not you.

☞ Who cares? It's your stepparent. Tell him or her you'd like a little more attention. Ask your real parent for help.

☞ You aren't their child. They have a special bond with their own kids, not you.

☞ Become friends with their kids.

☞ You can't compete with blood, so don't try and don't worry.

☞ This is what I say: "Hey, it wasn't my choice to live with you either, but as long as we're in this situation, we might as well try to get along."

☞ They are used to them, so they relate to them better.

☞ It takes time to adjust to a stepchild. But when they do, things will even out.

MY FAMILY IS PART FRENCH AND PART ENGLISH. ON MY FATHER'S SIDE, THEY ALL HAD DRINKING PROBLEMS AND FOUGHT A LOT.

ME AS A BABY

MY MOM'S PARENTS GOT DIVORCED WHEN SHE WAS SIX. HER FATHER LIVED IN LAS VEGAS IN A HOUSE HE'D PAINTED RED, WHITE, AND BLUE.

WHEN I WAS LITTLE, I LIVED WITH MY MOM AND DAD IN A BIG HOUSE. MY MOM HAD A ROSE GARDEN. MY DAD HAD BIRD FEEDERS. I HAD A TREE SWING. THE HOUSE HAD SPIDERS IN THE ATTIC.

WHEN I WAS FOUR, MY MOM AND DAD SEPARATED. THE JUDGE SAID MY DAD COULD SEE ME EVERY OTHER WEEKEND. MY DAD KNEW IT WAS THE RIGHT DECISION.

DAD WOULD NEVER HURT ME, BUT HE WAS AN ALCOHOLIC AND IT WAS BETTER NOT TO LIVE WITH HIM. MOM AND I MOVED TO THE CITY.

OUR APARTMENT WAS KINDA SMALL. MOM SAID THERE HAD TO BE CHANGES IN OUR LIVES. SHE SAID I MUST NOT LET ANYONE PUSH ME AROUND—MAYBE THAT'S THE WAY SHE FELT BULLIED BY DAD.

I LOVED THE CITY SCHOOL. MY FIRST FRIEND WAS ALICE. SHE WAS TOUGH, AND HER PARENTS WEREN'T EVEN DIVORCED. THEN SHE MOVED TO CHICAGO.

PUBLIC SCHOOL

EVENTUALLY, MY DAD WENT INTO A REHAB PROGRAM AND STOPPED DRINKING. ONCE HE GAVE ME A SALAMANDER THAT GOT LOOSE IN THE APARTMENT.

OVING

MY DAD'S A MUSICIAN.
SOMETIMES I STAY OUT
WITH HIM UNTIL
MIDNIGHT. IT MAKES ME
FEEL GROWN UP. LATE
FOR MY MOM IS 9 O'CLOCK.

HOLIDAYS ARE HARD. MY MOM
AND DAD QUARREL ABOUT WHO
GETS ME. I WENT TO MEXICO WITH
MY MOM. IT WAS FUN, BUT
I MISSED MY DAD, TOO.

NOW THAT I'M OLDER, I HAVE MORE
SAY. ONCE, I WENT TO EGYPT
WITH DAD. HE WANTED TO GO
TO THE PYRAMIDS. I WANTED TO
STAY IN THE HOTEL POOL.
HE DIDN'T LIKE THAT.

SOMETIMES MY DAD
LOSES HIS TEMPER, AND
THEN GIVES IN AND WANTS
ME TO SAY "I'M SORRY," TOO.
I DON'T LIKE IT WHEN
HE DOES THAT.

SMALL FIGHTS WITH DAD CAN TURN INTO GIANT BATTLES—LIKE IF I DON'T PUT LOTION ON MY BUG BITES. I'M NOT AS REBELLIOUS WITH MY MOM. IF I'M SICK, I STAY WITH HER.

WHEN THEY YELL AT ME, I TELL MYSELF THAT IT'S NOT THE END OF THE WORLD. I THINK, IF YOU HAVE CHILDREN, YOU SHOULDN'T YELL AT THEM.

MY DAD HAD A GIRFRIEND WHO DIDN'T LIKE THAT HE STOPPED DRINKING BECAUSE SHE DRANK, TOO. WHEN SHE TRIED TO DISCIPLINE ME, I IGNORED HER.

MY MOM'S BOYFRIEND TRIED TO DISCIPLINE ME TOO. BUT THAT'S NOT HIS JOB. ONLY YOUR OWN PARENTS SHOULD DISCIPLINE YOU.

ONCE I GOT UPSET BECAUSE MY DAD TOOK HIS GIRLFRIEND'S DAUGHTER TO A PLAY. MY MOM TOLD HIM I WAS MAD, AND THAT ENDED IT.

I HAD A NICE THERAPIST. SHE ASKED ME QUESTIONS LIKE "WHY WAS THE DUCK BOTH HAPPY AND SAD WHEN PEOPLE WERE MEAN TO HIM?"

MY MOM'S PREGNANT RIGHT NOW. SHE'S GETTING MARRIED SOON. I'M GOING TO BE THE BRIDESMAID. I DON'T KNOW IF I'LL BE JEALOUS OF MY NEW BROTHER OR SISTER.

MY MOM ONLY LETS ME WATCH AN HOUR OF TV A DAY. WITH MY DAD, I CAN WATCH LOTS. MY MOM DOESN'T MAKE ME EAT BROCCOLI. WITH MY DAD, I HAVE TO EAT BROCCOLI.

I DON'T WISH FOR MY PARENTS TO GET BACK TOGETHER AGAIN. I NEVER HAVE WISHED THAT. THEY DON'T GET ALONG ANYHOW.

s. mack

You learn how to get along with other people by what you see—good and bad—in your own family. Emily's divorced parents both love her a lot. They want to spend time with her. They want her to be happy. Sometimes, though, Emily sounds like she's being pulled between them. Her parents fight about things such as who sees her when. If they had plans in place that they could explain to her, it would make things easier.

It's common in families, especially ones with divorce, for the mom and dad to have different rules. It's also common for the adults and the children to have problems deciding who's in charge. Who is the boss, and what is your relationship to that person? Do you answer only to Mom? To Dad? To his or her boyfriend or girlfriend, too?

Rule Setter

Therapists often say, "The parent is the rule setter." That's probably what Emily heard from her therapist. But in real life the rules and ways of relating to one another are not that clear. At times Emily is probably alone with her future stepfather. Maybe she does something wrong, and he yells at her. He is an adult. He needs to be respected, even though his job is more to be a friend. To sort out who does what when, she should go to her parents.

Kids have to learn that adults make mistakes, too. When they do, they must be responsible for them and be disciplined.

Not all parents seem to take charge at home, and many, like Emily's, probably feel guilty about the divorce. They worry you're going to be ruined for life. To make up for that, they give you—the child—too much power and control.

Emily has had to struggle with a parent's addiction, fighting, and moves. But she seems strong and bold herself. When her dad takes his girlfriend's daughter someplace special, Emily has her mom tell him to stop. It might have been better for Emily to tell him herself. He may or may not change his behavior. He may even say, "When I take other people places, it doesn't mean I don't love you." But she also has to learn that even if you get mad, it won't always change the way a person acts. Emily is bright and lively. She'll understand.

KID PROBLEM, KID SOLUTIONS

What if my stepparent (or parent's boyfriend/girl-friend) puts down my other parent?

- Tell them that person is still your parent and they should treat them with respect.
- Put down someone close to them and ask them how it makes them feel.
- Tell your parent how you feel about it.
- Tell them you don't like it, and if that doesn't work, just ignore them.
- Let your parents handle it. It's their job anyway.
- Tell them it isn't fair. They don't know that parent well.
- Talk to them and the parent they're with—separately if necessary. They probably don't realize how much it hurts you.

I never went to day care. And I don't like school. I'm not good in it. Science and math are my worst subjects, probably 'cause I never listen. Usually I pass notes. What I really don't like, though, is the beginning of the year when the teacher asks, "How many people are in your family?"

I say, "Two," and the other kids laugh.

So what if I don't see my dad much? I don't think it's so bad. My time with him and Meredith, my stepmom, is every other weekend from six until ten on Friday and Saturday, and from ten to one on Sunday.

Afterward, when I come home, sometimes I go to my bedroom to think. I sit on my loft bed and look around—at my TV, my CD player, and my three dressers. I keep my Beanie Babies inside one of them, along with the Cabbage Patch doll my mom went all over town to find for me when I was little. I keep books in another dresser. One of my favorites is about how to keep friends, what to say to them, how to ask about their hobbies.

Bluer than Blue

When I'm bluer than blue, I daydream that I have a father around all the time. I think about having the most perfect family in the world: like, two parents and just me, the little angel in the house. The parents both get along really well. And they never yell at me either.

To get my mind off those thoughts, I start doing something else until the feeling passes over like a storm. I know my perfect family will probably never happen.

You know how when you're little, you don't know

what's going on? Well, I thought my dad completely left my mom when I was too young to know. I didn't even seriously know that I had a dad. I thought this guy that started showing up was just one of my mom's friends. I was surprised when he moved in with us.

Then they told me. He lived with us for a couple years, until I was about six. Then in the blink of an eye he left again. The best time I ever had with my dad was when he took me to a water park.

KID PROBLEM, KID SOLUTIONS

My dad/mom has been divorced more than once and is now married again. How do I get used to a new stepparent when I wasn't even used to the last one?

- ☞ Try what worked before.
- ☞ You always have your mom and dad, which is really what matters.
- ☞ Try to see this new person's good points. Tell yourself he or she makes your parent happy and that's what you want.
- ☞ Just go with the flow. You can't control what your parents do.
- ☞ Get used to the new one. You'll see the old one soon enough.
- ☞ Tell your mom or dad that you think they should settle down for good.
- ☞ Move in with another relative.
- ☞ Tell your parent that maybe they should see a therapist about why their relationships go wrong. Then look out. They may think you're trying to be smart.
- ☞ This is one of those things many kids have to put up with. Make the best of what you've got.
- ☞ Give this new person a chance, and it might get better.

Money

I'd have to say that money is a problem. Sometimes it seems we don't have any at all. My mom's gone back to school to try to get a better job that pays more. I wish she'd play the lotto, but she says that's not her style.

When I ask my dad for money, sometimes he gets mad just because of the question. Like, I wanted thirty dollars to get my hair permed. He and Meredith both work, so they could afford it. He kept putting it off, until finally I got one—but it didn't take.

My dad's always at work. Meredith is the one who watches me at their house. She's okay. Last week we worked in the backyard together pulling weeds.

She never had kids. That helps. She says I can tell her anything, and if I ask her not to, she won't tell anyone. She doesn't have any rules for me. They're all my dad's. I get away with stuff with my mom because she feels guilty. When my mom and I do get in fights, it's weird. I'm not used to yelling at girls. At school I yell at boys.

Last week I was upset with Mom. We fight about the stupidest things, like I have to vacuum practically every other day. I have to make my bed and clean my room. This time I didn't fold the laundry right. She yelled at me, and I yelled back. I called her names.

During my time at my dad's, when Meredith is making dinner, she has everything else off her mind. My dad is always late, so I say, "I want to move in with you."

She says, "Are you in a fight with your mom?"

"Yes," I say.

Then she says, "Well, you'll get in a fight with me and just want to go back to your mom."

That's probably true. Me and Meredith get in lots of fights. I have a bad temper. To get unmad, sometimes I pack up all my stuff and then pretend I forgot something so I can't leave. The four of us—me, Mom, Dad, and Meredith—never do anything together.

Leave Us Alone

We live in Ohio. My mom dated this guy that's in Chicago. They broke up. He was okay, but he just never showed up enough. He'd say stuff to my mom like, "I'll be here on your birthday." Then he couldn't make it. Whenever he came around, my mom would say, "Cici, you have to leave us alone." I'd go upstairs and try to forget about it.

"You're not going to have Mom all to yourself," I'd tell myself. "You have to live with that. You get her every day, except when she has that person over. And it's the same for Dad."

High Notes and Low Ones

I don't have dreams of getting married. When I realized I could sing good, I decided to be a singer. I'm scared to sing in front of my mom, but my friends are cool. I like to put on Celine Dion's CD and sing along with it. She can hit the high notes and the low ones.

If I'm at school or I'm feeling lonely, I sing. That's what gets me through. But you know what? I have to say for all the ups and downs, even though my mom and dad never really got married, I like the life I have.

There are a lot of unknowns about Cici; for example, what does "bluer than blue" mean? You can tell, though, she has questions about her dad. It would probably help if her mom let Cici know some of what went on between them. This man, her dad, shows up one day and is gone the next day. That's unsettling.

Some parents think it's best not to talk about this kind of thing, but a child starts wondering and worrying. The anxiety around the secret can become larger than the secret itself. It's okay for a child to ask parents for information. And it's okay to have this conversation more than once. What parents tell you when you're six years old is different from what they tell you when you're ten. You hear more details.

Intact Family

Cici's daydream about the wonderful intact family—Mom, Dad, and her—is normal. But what can happen is that you begin to believe that an intact family is the best. And you think that if only you could be part of an intact family, your life would be perfect. This just isn't true.

Dealing with parents' dating can be tricky. Some parents think, "I'll protect my children. I won't let them see me date." That can work, unless they suddenly pop this person into their kids' lives. For Cici, a boyfriend shows up and her mother sends her off to her room. It's better if a new person is introduced slowly, with the three of them doing things together first.

In a lot of ways Cici and her mother have a normal

parent-child relationship. Still, her mom has the stress of being a single parent. She probably feels she's done something bad to Cici, and she tries to make up for it by not setting and enforcing many rules.

Meanwhile, Cici worries about being loyal to her mom, even as she asks her stepmother, Meredith, about moving in. Meredith is good. She's not trying to be Cici's mom or to bad-mouth Cici's mom. That can happen when stepparents aren't comfortable in their role. Lots of kids fear they're being disloyal to the biological parent if they like the Merediths in their lives. Really, there's enough love to go around.

Cici has friends. She's outgoing and talented. These are signs of health. The children who withdraw and shut down are the ones to worry about most.

KID PROBLEM, KID SOLUTIONS

What person, program, or thing has helped you the most in getting through all these changes?

☞ My aunt Carole and Snuffles, my stuffed animal, helped me most.

☞ My diary helps me explain these shocks to myself.

☞ An anger management class has shown me ways to calm down when I get upset about the changes.

☞ Therapy helped me the most.

☞ Anyone who's close to you can help. You'll get through it. All your parents want is for you and them to be happy.

-ǒ-

What do you know now about separation/divorce/remarriage that you wish you had known in the beginning?

☞ If you don't like the new stepparent, tell your parent before the marriage, not after, when it's too late for sure.

☞ You're not the only one going through a divorce. You're not the only one wanting to have a mom and dad together. Your friends are there for you, even if it's just to listen.

☞ If you come from a big family, like me, you can always find support when you most need it.

☞ Sometimes you have to be your own best friend to get through this. Worse things can happen than divorce.

Chapter 4

Talking about your problems can act like a safety valve. It lets out the steam. But for talking to work best you need at least two people—you and a thoughtful listener. This isn't always possible.

For some, writing is the answer. Writing is private. It's you and your heart. Just putting words on paper helps make sense of the world around you. You write when you're crying to stop the tears. You write when you're mad to decrease the rage. You write when you're confused to find out why.

Some of you write regularly about what troubles you. You forget about perfect spelling and punctuation. Instead you write with passion and intensity—until you're tired.

Experts agree. This practice is beneficial. They

say what's best is to write out your worries for fifteen to twenty minutes for three or four days in a row. Afterward you feel better emotionally, and physically, too.

For this book students from New York to Texas to California volunteered to write or draw about how their lives have collided with divorce and remarriage. Some filled a page. Some finished a paragraph. Some took it as an assignment and spent several days writing, sketching, drawing, and rewriting.

UNSENT LETTERS AND
SCREAMING MATCHES

In the end most agreed you can take sad feelings and turn them into something positive—a poem, a family portrait, an essay on splitting up. Some preteens and teenagers write letters to family members. They know conversations can blow up into screaming matches; with letters you don't have to send them. It's the writing that helps. Writing helps you face what's happening in order to move on.

From the range of student responses comes the following collection. The essays are usually shortened. The poetry and art are unchanged. They are roughly divided into three sections: separation, divorce, and remarriage.

Read what your peers have to say. Look at their drawings. Put yourself in their place and think whether you'd have the same reactions. Then take a pen and paper to a quiet corner, the place you feel most comfortable . . . and try it yourself.

> **separation:** to break apart, disconnect, divide, sever, detach, split up; to cease to live together as husband and wife

Ray, age fifteen:

The head in Ray's drawing has no ears. Do you think this means he didn't want to hear what his parents had to say about their separation?

Marvin, age fourteen:

WHY!

Can't you see the pain
I feel?
I cried at night not
Knowing why you had to
Leave me.
Was it because I got bad grades
Or because I misbehave?
Why can't you just come back home?
I will never do good
If I have to be on my own.

Lola, age twelve:

Six months ago my dad told my mom he just didn't love her anymore. They've been separated ever since. They aren't divorced, because my mom says Dad can't afford it. Plus, he is a big procrastinator. My mom cries and worries a lot. My older brother acts like he doesn't care. My younger sister doesn't understand. A few weeks ago my dad moved two hundred miles away. He called once, but he has bills here he hasn't paid.

Yusef, age twelve:

My parents are separated, but they live in the same house in different rooms. My mom is loving, in some ways overly loving. But my dad isn't. He's hardly ever home and gets angry when he is. Like, sometimes he explodes and throws stuff at the wall for no reason. Then other times he cries when I say, "Could you help me with my school assignment?" We used to be silly together, joking around, wrestling. Now watching him is like watching someone die.

Clarissa, age fourteen:

My parents separated a year and a half ago. My dad is manic-depressive and always refused to get help. My parents were married for about five years before I was born. My mom considered divorcing my dad during that time. She thought a baby—me—would change things.

It didn't work. My dad became verbally abusive. It spread from my mother to me. After one last chance for the gazillionth time, my mother told Dad she was leaving him. My dad decided he wanted to be the first out the door, so we were forced to deal with his leaving. I knew, though, it was for the best.

Everything would be okay if he would deal with the fact that they aren't going to get back together. He still begs for forgiveness. Now I have to see him every Sunday in church, and it's my mom who looks worse for being the divorcer. She just began the divorce process. I agree with her, but I still want a relationship with my dad.

Logan Chestnut, age nine,
Brookwood Elementary School, Snellville, Georgia:

TEARS

My mom cries sometimes
For some reason.
I think it's because
Of my dad
Who kind of blows by
Like a season.

Ivy, age thirteen:

I have older and younger half brothers. It's weird not having any real brothers or sisters. My mom and my older brother's biological father were together for a couple months. When she got pregnant, he left and didn't come back until the very day she was in the hospital. "I'm getting married this afternoon," he told her. I feel bad for my brother. His dad's a jerk.

Then there's me. My mom and my father were together two years before I came along. He and my mom broke up a year later, and they had a custody battle. My mom got custody. My dad was allowed to see me on weekends. But instead I haven't seen him since I don't remember.

When I'm older, I am going to look for him. I wonder if we think alike and things like that. Then there's my little brother. My mom and his father were married for six years. Now they're separated. My brother is the only one who still sees him. He never adopted my older brother or me. My mother and stepfather always fought, so I'm glad they separated. It's okay for me. I've had a lot of practice getting through all this.

David, age eight:

My life was ruined by the divorce, but from it another me was born. And the new me is one cool person.

---

divorce: to terminate, dissolve, divide, split; to legally end a marriage

Nanette, age sixteen:

UNTIL TOMORROW

Sit,
   LISTEN
      Hear our stories . . .
each different in its own respect
each linked by a single thread
   D
      I
         V
            O
               R
                  C
                     E
   like a whisper
      haunting and scary
   whimpers, cries, screams
Buried anger,
                  death within the soul
Broken home,
               broken heart.

Michael Cope, age nine,
Brookwood Elementary School, Snellville, Georgia:

Divorce feels like you're being shot with a gun. All your blood
is pushing out of you, you're losing your loved ones, and your
heart is breaking. While I was watching TV, my mom and dad
called me to come to their room. I didn't know what was happening. I thought maybe it was good until I saw their watery

eyes. "Michael," they said, "we are getting a divorce." I didn't know what to say. All that came out were my own tears.

Now that the divorce has been over for a while, things are back to normal. I still see my mom and dad, but both of them started seeing other people. It's not so bad, except who Mom sees is not my dad and who Dad sees is not my mom. So it's not the same. I learned you never forget the day the divorce happens. But you get used to things. You survive.

Hillary, age ten:

My parents have recently gone through a divorce. They got married too quickly, and they have opposite personalities. But I never thought they'd break up. They never fought, plus we'd just built a big house. They didn't cheat on each other either. Only love disappeared. I'm scared now because my future seems like a giant question mark.

Alex, age eleven:

My dad was an alcoholic and would beat all of us. He was nicer to me because right before I was born, he broke his leg. He had to stay home to take care of me. He got to know me better.

Once he beat my mother until she almost died. Whenever she left him, he'd send her flowers. When she came back, it would start all over. When I was seven, they divorced. I see him every once in a while. I feel sorry for him. He doesn't have much money, and he feels terrible about what he did. After they divorced, my dad realized what he lost. He apologized to my brother and me. I started crying.

Simon, age fourteen:

When a divorce occurs, the children are often the ones who carry the consequences. In this case the kid feels trapped in his parents' situation. He feels depressed, and the world shows him the wrong way out—drugs, alcohol, or even suicide. He is very confused.

Kerri, age twelve:

Divorce has been a big thing in my life. My parents divorced when I was six. I didn't even know what was going on. We just moved, and my dad didn't come along. So much pressure is put on you when your parents are divorced. When I was younger, it was decided that I would live with my mother. However, in the past four years my father has been trying to get custody of my brother and me. I always worry about upsetting my parents. I don't want to do something wrong and have one of them hate me. I am so afraid of failing them. Because of the divorce I worry about my performance in school and everything else.

Shawnee, age fifteen:

It's hard when your mom or dad starts dating. I hated my mom's boyfriend for the longest time. I felt myself competing with him for her attention. After a while I got to know and love him. Now we're great friends. After all the hardship I thought things would get worse, but they got better. My advice to someone going through similar problems is to take each day as it comes. Try to understand and try to keep talking with all your family.

Case, age eleven:

My mom chose bad boyfriends. There were two of them that would yell and hit me. I never had to decide which parent to live with because finally neither of them were around. I live with my grandparents. They're the most important people in my life. I wish I'd never lived with either parent. To other kids with divorced parents, do the best you can with the life you have. Stay in school and make yourself proud.

Skye, age twelve:

Eight years ago, when I was four, my dad left and never looked back. My mom has told me stories and shown me pictures of him. But I don't know the man, and because of that I don't think I know myself. My life is a mystery. I want to discover who I am and close this chapter. In a way, though, I am thankful. My dad made me understand that even when people leave and don't come back, you have to go on with your life.

Megan Raym␣␣r, age fourteen,
Argo Community High School, Summit, Illinois:

WONDERING AND WISHING

When you left her so long ago
There was one less person you never got to know.
But do you even care about her?
Do you wonder what she's like?
Do you wish you were there when she . . .
Took her first step, spoke her first word,
Learned how to ride a bike?
Do you ever ask how old is she now,
What color are her eyes,
How long is her hair, and does she tell lies?
What is her favorite color,
What does she do for fun,
And will she go to college when high school is done?
Well, she is fourteen,
Her eyes are blue,
She has long blond hair, and is honest and true.
Her favorite color is green,
She plays games for fun,
And she will go to college when high school is done.
There is one more thing I would like to add,
That she is me and I wonder about you,
Dad.

Laura, age fourteen:

I live with my mother and brother. My parents separated when
I was six. My father is gay and lives with his partner and an

adopted child, my half? step? sister. I love all my family members very much. On weekends and during the summer my brother and I spend time at our dad's house.

At first when they divorced, I was angry with my parents. I wanted them to get back together. But starting shortly after the separation, mom had a live-in boyfriend. Then after a couple years they split up, too. That was hard on me, and I made it hard for my mother. I'm fourteen now. Looking back, I think counseling could have helped me.

I've never had a problem with my dad's situation. But because it could threaten his job, he's not openly gay. And that means I have to be pretty silent. I've had to learn to deal with the insults about gays and lesbians from kids at school. I'd gladly tell people the truth, despite what it could mean to my reputation. I've considered all this. For my father's sake I have only told my closest friends.

Gia, age ten:

My parents just got divorced this year. We were never a real family anyway. We never did things together. If my parents were around each other, they were fighting. Sometimes it got so bad that one of them would leave for the night. Sometimes my brother would leave, too.

I like it better now without the fighting. I have a much happier and stronger relationship with each of my parents. My brother has helped me a lot by always being there for me.

> *[re]marriage:* to unite [again] in a close relationship; to join together [again]; the institution where a loving couple weds [again] in a special ceremony

I don't think the divorce has affected my life forever the way some people say.

Amanda, age eleven:

I would not have gotten through any of this divorce without God. He has been my Father, my protector, and my comforter. If I had not known him during these times, if he had not put his arms of love around me, I would not be here. I don't know why he allows certain things to happen to us, but I do know that his love is everlasting. He will never leave or forsake us. He is my life, and I thank him for being by my side through life's storms.

Owen, age nine:

I feel I'm growing up in Splitsville. Most of my family, even my grandparents, and most of my friends' families are divorced. My parents have stupid fights over custody. I live with my mom. My bossy brothers live with my dad, his wife, and my half sister. I like it that way. I think when you say your wedding vows—"till death do you part"—you should live up to them.

Lilly, age ten:

I have two families. One family is my mom, Mom's boyfriend, his three girls, three dogs, and my real little sister. She has a mind of her own. She's stubborn, and she never left the "terrible twos." My other family is my dad, stepmom, half sister, and stepbrother. I love both my mom and my dad. I usually get along with my mom's boyfriend's girls. I love my half sister, but my stepmother won't let me hold her. My stepmom is pregnant again. My stepbrother is in the same grade as me. My life is fine.

Alonzo, age fifteen:

My parents' relationship was fine until I was born. Then everything changed. My stupid father didn't want me, and he was going to leave my mother if I was born. He told my mother she would do better without me. But you know what? My mom didn't care what he said or what he did. She told him she was going to have me no matter what. So my dad left her and I was born.

As I grew up she told me what happened. It doesn't bother me much, but what does hurt is my father not wanting me. Why didn't he love me just like my mom did? Why couldn't they stay together and be a family? Now I am living with my mother and my stepfather. He cares about me and has raised me since I was one year old.

Kristi, age thirteen:

My parents divorced when I was four years old and my younger sister was eighteen months old. However mean it may seem, the divorce was great for my family. My father was an addict. After they divorced, he moved away and bounced from rehab to rehab. While this was going on, my mom remarried. My stepdad is the greatest man alive. His daughter lives with us, and now I have two baby sisters, who are beyond beautiful. So even though my family began with many problems, things are wonderful now. My dad moved back about three years ago. My sister and I think he might be back to his old ways, but there is only so much you can do for a person. He's a grown man; it's up to him.

Wendy, age twelve:

Last year on my eleventh birthday my family and I were at the world's biggest mall. In this one store my brother and I saw a cool computer game with a sign saying, MEET THE INVENTOR. I wanted Mom to buy me the game, so we went looking for her. When I told her what I wanted, she refused.

Later Mom told us she had been married to the game's inventor. What?! I knew nothing about this, and she sprang it on me just like that. It weirded me out that my mom had this totally different secret life. For all I know, she could be some other kid's mother, too. I'd like to think I know my mother, but after that experience I don't know. But still, she's my mother and I love her.

Max, age eight:

I took a kite. I covered it with tinfoil. Now it's a shield, and I can even roll it up. When bad things happen—like my stepmom yells at me, my half brother bugs me, I forget my homework at my mom's—I unroll my shield. I hold it in front of me and tell myself that it keeps the bad things from getting inside me. It works. I calm down.

Chapter 5

The Other Side of the Marriage-Divorce Line

This book focuses on preteens and teenagers living with divorce and/or remarriage. But some members of intact families say so much time is spent looking at divorce, people forget to look at together marriages. There can be misunderstanding on both sides of the marriage-divorce line. And much can be learned, too.

Those head-deep in divorces, parents' dating, trips between homes, and stepfamily adjustments think only someone with similar problems can understand their feelings. At a time when everyone may need a listener, these beliefs can disrupt friendships and cause more pain.

Here are the words and pictures of students whose mom and dad have remained married. Some of their insights may comfort you. Some may anger you. Some may even surprise you. All of them show you a glimpse inside intact families.

PERFECT SUGAR-COATED FAMILIES?

Sharicka, age ten:

We pay so much attention to the children of divorced parents. I'd like to know if there are others like me—the one from the "perfect, sugar-coated" family, trying to be a friend to a girl who thinks I could never understand.

Taylor, age nine:

My parents have been married for twelve years. I don't believe they have ever been happy. I wish they'd get a divorce. Some people tell me it's 100 percent better. Some people tell me it's horrible. In my eyes I don't think it would be so bad. My parents would be happier, and my mom and I would have the money that my dad now uses to buy cigarettes and lottery tickets. That's what's tearing my family apart.

Billy, age fifteen:

Billy first drew his father's arm outstretched pointing a gun at his wife. He erased this, but in the original art you can still see the outline.

Malik, age sixteen:

I feel that divorce is not an option. It is just an excuse. The husband or wife is not "man" or "woman" enough to cope with their problems. Life revolves around family. Love and joy fuel it. Divorce affects all family members. It breaks people apart.

Kalynn, age ten:

I live with my mom; dad; brother; dog, Zinger; and two chinchillas. I know divorce hurts, but just because your parents are married, like mine, it doesn't mean you get to be with them all the time. My brother and I get home from school at 3:00 P.M. Since my dad is at work, my mom takes us to our older sister's, and then she goes to work. Mom gets done at 9:00 P.M. and comes to my sister's. We stay there until 10:00 P.M., when we go pick up Dad. By the time we get home, it is 11:00 P.M. My brother and I go straight to bed and get up at 6:00 A.M. to catch the bus. My brother and I hardly ever see our mom and dad unless it's some huge holiday.

Steven, age sixteen:

My parents did not get divorced. My father passed away. Before he died, he told me to let my mom meet new people. I said, "Sure," but when she finally did, it was weird to see her with another man, especially so soon after my dad's death. I didn't like him. I thought my mom was too good for him. And I was left at home with my brothers and my sister while they went out.

We needed her. We were angry, and she didn't even know. She was in "la-la land." One day she said, "Steven, you've been acting differently. What's wrong?"

I answered, "Many things that you don't notice." Finally I told her I felt like she had turned her back on us kids. All I wanted was for her to tell us everything was going to be all right. That she would never leave our side.

That was two years ago. Today things are a lot better. It took a long time, but now I realize my mom needed someone to pay attention to her and tell her the same thing we wanted to hear: Soon life will be fine.

Emerald, age fifteen:

My parents are together, but my cousin's aren't. She was nine when her parents got divorced. At first it didn't affect her, but when she became a teenager, the problems started. She threatened to run away, because she felt nobody loved her. She told me she put all her trust in her parents and they betrayed her by going their separate ways. She wanted to isolate herself from her family.

At school she tries not to show her depression. She's a quiet person and knows how to keep her feelings inside. Slowly, though, she wants to change. She wants to try harder in school. When she feels the anger coming, she tries to block it out of her mind by playing basketball for hours. It gives her time to calm down and think, she says. It's working. She is improving.

Kara, age thirteen:

Zoe, my best friend since third grade, and her parents are going through a divorce. She, another friend of ours, and I had a sleepover. It got emotional. Zoe said she feels the separation is her fault; that she's the unwanted child.

See, her parents had a daughter, and then they lost the boy that came afterward. Zoe was born, and three years later another boy was born. Because her sister was the first child, her mother has a special place for her. Because the next child was a boy, he became her dad's favorite. So she feels like she is the problem.

My family is close. Sometimes it's even hard for me to listen to Zoe's problems. I'm trying to be a good friend, but I'm not good at giving advice. It's not that I can't speak from my heart. It's that I can't translate what I feel. She worries me, and I feel like I can't help.

Sally, age fifteen:

My best friend, Tracy, is not as fortunate as me. Her parents divorced when she was little. It changed her in many ways. She needed a father figure. Her mother remarried, and Tracy's mom stopped giving her the attention she needed.

She was more like the adult, and her mom was more like the child. I think it made a difference in Tracy's life. It changed the way she looked at the world. There is so much out there, but nobody showed her.

I'm proud of Tracy. Today she is more adult and has taught herself everything she knows. She is not only just like a sister to me, but also someone I admire. If you ever need someone to talk to, your best friend is always there, just like Tracy and me. My advice to kids would be: Don't get yourself down because your mom and dad aren't together. It doesn't mean they don't have feelings for you.

Chapter 6

The Answer, and Real-Life Happy Endings

Before writing this book, I collected the thoughts of more than a thousand preteens and teenagers. What they had in common were lives touched by divorce and remarriage. In the preceding chapters were samples of their voices.

I read all those stories over again, along with the ones that for various reasons I left out. They described similar issues. They felt like the Ping-Pong ball hit by battling parents. They couldn't understand their parents' dating choices. Or in general they came up with the same ideas of how to explain these life changes to themselves.

In the end my goal was to answer the question asked by sixth and seventh graders in this book's introduction:

The Question

When divorce and remarriage collide with your life, are you doomed to an unhappy future, or can you pick up life's pieces, put them together, and successfully move on?

DIVORCE HURTS . . . BUT

While one answer doesn't fit all lives, after hearing and reading what everyone had to say, I found this to be the most typical answer: Divorce hurts. In fact, it can hurt so much you feel shot in the head and the heart in a single moment. But the answer is just as clear.

The Answer

Living through divorce does not automatically cause wounds that never heal. It does not have to be the end of your world. Like a giant puzzle, the pieces of your life can be arranged and rearranged into a vibrant picture. You can learn from your experiences, grow emotionally, and have a happy future.

How does this happen? What makes the difference? A parent or two, and you.

How parents deal with the changes created by a divorce or remarriage makes a huge difference in how well you—their child—do in life. To the best of their ability, if your mother, your father, or, one hopes, both of them remain grown-ups, you're already heading in the right direction. Let's start with that rule and go on to some others.

☞ Mom and Dad remain grown-ups.

☞ They allow you to remain the child.

☞ They don't confide their adult feelings and secrets to you.

☞ They don't put each other down in front of you.

☞ They don't make you carry Mom/Dad messages that make you feel uncomfortable.

☞ They answer your questions about custody, money, where you will live when, etc., when you ask them.

☞ They let you know that the emotions you feel—from anger to sadness to confusion—are normal and tell you what to do about them.

☞ They reach out to individuals and groups (relatives, school and community programs, on-line resources, religious organizations, therapists, neighbors, etc.) who can offer your family advice, support, and information.

☞ They remain emotionally and physically available to you.

☞ When appropriate, they listen to your opinions and solutions to divorce and remarriage problems.

WHAT ABOUT YOU?

You, too, play an important role in creating a happy ending. Divorce and remarriage have hit you hard. How you act and react is a vital part of the picture.

Life isn't always easy or fair. Not everybody has parents who can follow even one or two of these rules. What if the parent raising you drinks or drugs too much; abuses you physically, emotionally, or sexually; neglects you; has a history of serious medical or mental problems requiring hospitalization; can't begin to handle the divorce him- or herself, to the point that that parent seems to vanish emotionally?

You're a child afloat in an adult world. You may even be responsible for younger brothers and sisters. This is too much for you to accomplish. Look for at least one, and if possible more, wise and trusted adults to turn to. Tell them you need help getting through these enormous life changes. You can't do it on your own.

This person could be a relative, a friend's parent, a longtime family friend, a teacher, a preacher, a counselor, a youth worker, a coach, or a community leader. Keep looking until you feel you're getting the best advice and comfort available. Don't give up. There is always some positive person willing to hold on to you in bleak weather. The hard part is finding the right one.

Maybe, though, your life isn't that complicated. Yes, you are angry, depressed, or shut down. In turn you blame all your problems on the divorce's fallout. That's understandable. Life as you know it changed, and through no fault of yours. It's not fair. You could call it adult selfish. You don't have a lot of say-so in the matter.

Still, remaining mad, bewildered, and thrown by the changes isn't healthy either. Your parents didn't decide to divorce or remarry just to make you miserable. There were and are reasons. You may not accept them, but these adult decisions are not made without pain on your parents' part. Problems and issues you don't understand now may make sense as you get older.

Time after time, those preteens and teenagers I talked to told me that at a certain point they decided they were old enough to make peace with these changes. They were not powerless. They had some control. There were, they realized, kids'-eye-view solutions to divorce's problems that they could try. And if their first attempts didn't work, they would just keep trying.

CAN'T TALK, CAN'T WRITE, CAN'T DRAW

You need to find a healthy way to let out the emotions caused by divorce and remarriage. If you don't, the pain only increases. To numb yourself, you may start doing such unhealthy things as developing an eating disorder, joining a gang, or self-mutilating.

In the earlier chapters preteens and teens showed the value of talking, writing, and drawing out their problems. But even those outlets don't work for everyone.

It's up to you, then, to look in your heart and decide what's the best safety valve for you. Maybe it's sports. Run, play ball, shoot baskets, swim until you feel the tension diminish. Or what about computer games? Music? Volunteer work? Hobbies? Religion? Focus on whatever positive effort gets you through your tough moments.

In this book you heard girls and boys talk about their pain and their own search for solutions. Some of them still felt stuck and overwhelmed by troubles. But for others, you read what worked for them in moving on to a bright future. There are no "Ten Easy Steps to Surviving Divorce and Remarriage." But dozens of steps and answers do exist. Pick and choose from that advice until you discover something that seems the right fit for you.

For the next half hour put aside thoughts of your own and your family's pain. Instead concentrate on your future. Imagine how you would like your life to be when you turn seventeen. Do some realistic dreaming.

Two final speakers want to share their experiences with you. Think of them as an older sister and brother. They hope that from them you'll gain strength and inspiration. Think of them and think of your own new beginnings.

NOW YOU SEE HIM, NOW YOU DON'T, NOW YOU SEE HIM . . .

Written by Susana "Susy" Robledo, age seventeen,
Argo Community High School, Summit, Illinois

Part I, Zero to Six

I was about two and a half years old when my parents separated. What made it even sadder was my mom was pregnant with my baby brother, Tony.

Christmas Day four years later I was upstairs at my cousin Maria's apartment. "Susy, Susy," Tony started yelling. "There's some guy downstairs with presents for us!"

"What guy?"

"I don't know. I've never seen him before."

When I got to the door—what a surprise—it was my dad! This was the first time we had heard from him since the separation. And this was the first time my brother had ever met our father.

My eyes filled with tears. I ran up and gave him a big kiss. I didn't ask him why he hadn't come around in such a long time. I could only think about how happy I was to see him. I was hoping that now he'd be with us often.

Forgotten Existence—Flashback

Seeing him soon becomes like a dream. Six months go by. There are no phone calls, no letters, no visits. Has he disappeared off the face of the earth or just forgotten our existence? Then suddenly in July my mother is handing me the phone. It's my dad's voice saying, "Hi, baby, how are you?"

"Fine," I respond with a smile on my face.

"Well, tomorrow I'm taking you swimming." I'm so excited, I almost can't stand.

My mom takes the phone and says to him, "Why did you tell her that? You bring her hope and then break her heart. You better be here."

The next morning I'm up before anybody else. "Mommy, get up," I say, trying to drag her out of bed. "My daddy's coming any minute."

"Not yet, Susy. He won't be here until the afternoon."

"Mommy, please, I have to get ready now or I'm going to miss him when he comes."

I put on my swimsuit, my shorts and sandals. My mom packs the rest of my stuff in a bag. I run to the window and sit on my stool. By eleven o'clock there's still no sign of him.

"Susy, come eat," says my mom.

I don't leave the window. I'm afraid I might miss him.

That night I'm so upset I go to bed without eating. I don't hear from him again for a long time.

BAD AND GOOD THINGS ABOUT DIVORCE

Paul, age eight:
Bad: You're uncomfortable when someone asks about the missing parent.
Good: You can get out of trouble because you have a good excuse, the divorce.

Part II, Seven to Twelve

My mother has always worked. Thank God my grandmother was there. She even let us live with her. The only problem was the apartment had just one bedroom. For many years the four of us were crammed in there like kids.

When I was about nine and Tony was six, my mom told us she'd gone to court and divorced Dad. I cried, but Tony had no reaction. After all, he didn't even know our father. "Does this mean Daddy doesn't love me anymore?" I asked my mother. I'd always thought if you love your kids, you'll be there for them no matter what. She didn't answer.

That same year, though, Mom told us that Dad would be giving us a ride to school every morning. Amazingly, he showed up. "Why don't you come see us?" I finally got to ask.

"Your grandmother threw me out. Your mom wouldn't let me visit you," he said.

I knew my grandma called him "that lazy bum." He'd say he'd look for a job, and every day he'd come home with the same story: No one would hire him. I was little. I believed him. After four days of taking us to school, he was gone again without a word. He couldn't last a week.

I said to my mom, "Why did you and my dad get divorced?"

"Well," she said, "the day I told him I was pregnant with Tony, he said, 'Get an abortion or I'll leave.' I showed him the door." I was proud of my mom and disgusted with my father.

Part III, Thirteen to Now

In my family it's tradition to have a Mass and a big party to celebrate a girl turning fifteen and becoming a young lady. This party is expensive and many people contribute. I decided, Why not ask Dad? By then he owned a landscaping business. He had the money.

When he said no, I gave him a piece of my mind. It wasn't the party. It was all those years he never sent a dime. Tony and I had been cut short of many things. If we wanted something expensive, like a bike, Mom had to work extra hours. That also meant no other luxuries, like going to the movies, until she got back on her feet.

My father was quiet. Then he told me he had to go. I called him a few days later. He'd had his phone disconnected. The next time we heard from him was a year later. He said to my mom, "If Susy and Tony want to see me, they better call right away. I'm leaving town."

Danielle, age ten:
Bad: You want to do something with friends, but you have to go to your other parent's house.
Good: Your stepparent may have a special skill, like computers, and teach you.

I was furious, but Tony did call him. The next morning he took us to breakfast. Even though he looked at us as if he loved and missed us, I didn't buy it. After all those years, he thought he could come into our life and pretend that all that had happened never happened? Plus, he said he wanted us to meet his two other kids. This set me off.

"How come you don't send Mom any child support for us?"

"I don't have a lot of money," he said.

"How can you afford to have two other children and travel? How did you afford to buy your new Camaro?"

"You're just like your mother," he said.

"She's the one that raised me, didn't she? So how many other kids do you have?"

"I don't know," he answered.

"How can you not know? How can you not care? How can you afford to have kids if you don't even support the first two you brought into the world? That is, if we are the first ones!"

He knew now I wasn't going to believe what he said anymore. I was proud of myself for speaking the questions that had been in my heart for so many years. It no longer mattered that he had no answers.

The Worst to the Best

I'm seventeen now and Tony's almost fourteen. We never heard from my father again. I don't miss him or care to see him. We've made it without him in the past. We'll make it without him in the future.

We're finally moving out of our tiny apartment. Mom bought a house. We're excited. I thank my grandmother for being there for us, and my mother, whom I love more than words can say. I thank her for being strong and doing everything she could so we always had what we really needed.

And to everyone going through what I did, I want to tell you: Hang in there. Sometimes you have to go through the worst to get to the best.

THE CHOICE

Interview with Keith Brian Kurman, age seventeen, Wallkill Senior High School, Wallkill, New York

Divorce doesn't have to be a bad thing for kids. Trust me. I know. I've been through it. From elementary school to now not many of my friends' parents have been divorced.

They ask me, "Are you scarred for life? What about all the fights?"

I say, "I don't know what you're talking about. My parents are best friends." I love being able to say that.

This Thanksgiving my stepmom's brother was sick. She had to be with him. That meant my dad came to our house. I looked around the table and there were both my parents, my stepdad, my sister, my twin stepbrothers, my half brother, and my stepgrandparents, whom I consider my grandparents. Then my real grandparents stopped by. We'll do the same thing Christmas Eve.

We all value the family. That has nothing to do with divorce and remarriage. We have these cool family traditions. For example, on your first birthday you get a "mess cake." I have pictures of me covered with cake, making a nice mess on myself. The oldest family member gives the baby's first haircut. If you're eating anything and find a toothpick, you get to kiss the cook.

A Rabbi and a Minister

My dad's Jewish. My mom's Methodist. She told me that when my dad brought her home to meet his parents the first time, his mother was a little shocked she wasn't Jewish. My grandfather was watching a Yankees game. No one bothered him during a game. He looked up and said, "Let the kid"—my future dad—"do what he wants." Case closed.

A rabbi and a minister married them. Some of my earliest memories are of having Passover with my dad's parents and Easter with my mom's. I loved doing Hanukkah and Christmas. I learned a lot from my grandparents. They wanted me to be involved with them, in religion and in life.

Jody, age eleven:
Bad: You slack off in school and start doing badly.
Good: You get more brothers and sisters.

My dad's dad and I had this wonderful, weird connection. He was hilarious. Everyone loved him. I remember spending time in their little apartment. After he died, my grandmother, a shrimp of a lady but tough, would walk me around their neighborhood. No one touched her.

On my mom's side there was my great-grandmother, called Mama. She always brought her bread pudding, my dad's favorite, to family functions. My grandparents, Pa and Nana, are still alive. When I was a kid, Pa called me Mighty Mouse. Even now Nana cooks me my favorite birthday treat, an outrageous vanilla cake with peanut butter icing. How could I not love them? On both sides I feel totally surrounded by a warm, happy family.

Words I Understood

I was six when my parents told me they were leaving each other. They used words I understood. They loved each other. They just couldn't live together. I never saw the inside of a courtroom with a black-robed judge saying, "There's a battle going on."

Dad lived in the house with my sister and me. Mom lived a few blocks away. We still saw both of them. Together they still made decisions about us, including holding me back in first grade. They thought it would help me if I stayed in my same spot.

Even as time went by and my mom was with a new person, Joe, I didn't think, "Oh, my parents are divorced." I thought, "Mom and Dad still see each other." And they did. What can I say? I was little and wasn't paying attention.

When my mom got remarried, I thought it was nice. I got to be the ring bearer. I remember sitting at the bar with Joe, the man who would be my stepfather in a couple hours. My mom was late. Joe was mumbling, "She's not coming. She's not coming."

I looked at him and said, "Do you think she's going to leave me here with you?" He laughed. An hour and a half later my mom showed up with a car-wouldn't-start story.

My sister and I are eight years apart. She was a teenager then. I remember her fighting with my mom and dad. I think she blamed one or the other for the divorce. She knew the meaning of divorce in a way I didn't have a clue.

From the day she could walk, she was independent. Mom would pick out an outfit for her to wear; she'd put on a different one. Still, she's sensitive and compassionate. My mom and Joe bought a house, and we decided to go live with them. It was okay with my dad. He had just started to see this woman, Suzanne. When they got married, to me it just seemed like I had an even bigger family. Cool.

Fear of Fighting

My parents talk all the time. I've seen them bicker at work about family business, but that's about it. In fact, they say "I love you" to each other. As I've gotten older I've wondered whether my dad has a fear of fighting. He's quick to make up. I'm more opinionated with him. He's not going to get mad at me for things that might make my mom angry. And there are whole conversations I've had with one that I wouldn't have with the other. That's an unexpected benefit of divorce. You can trust one parent not to tell the other what you've said.

A time or two I started to ask my mother, "Don't you think the divorce was more surprising to me because you didn't scream at each other?" But before she could answer, I stopped her. Our lives work the way they are. I leave well enough alone. I don't want to change them.

I walk into my dad's house, and after the 152-pound black Labrador jumps all over me, my twin stepbrothers say, "Keith, come help us with our homework. Check out this new game we got." They look up to me. My half brother and I adore each other.

BAD AND GOOD THINGS ABOUT DIVORCE

Zina, age eleven:
Bad: You don't get as much attention.
Good: The utility bills are cheaper.

I love that I see both my parents on holidays. I'm never torn. In fact, I see them equally all the time. They never make me feel odd about the divorce. I have my own room at each house. And it's *my* room, not some spare room. I have a full bedroom set in each place. I have a futon, and it's always down unless I have company.

My room at my mom's house is probably more me. I spend

more time there. I have one of those sling chairs, a TV, my die-cast car collection. Basically the room is like a little apartment. And in each bedroom, in each house, I feel at home. I usually carry an overnight duffel bag full of clothes. Then I can make spur-of-the-moment decisions where I'll spend the night.

I learned, too, that what works for me is to think of my step-parents as another mom and dad. It's made my world larger. Like, my dad's not much into hunting or sports. My stepdad helped me shoot my first gun. He got me the basketball hoop.

I'm a big kid. I wanted to play football. My stepgrandfather coached peewee. My dad refused to let me play; he thought it was too violent. We had an argument. For the first time I used the divorce to get something I wanted. In the end I never played football. I decided my need to play was less important than how much it would upset my dad. Instead I ended up becoming a class officer and chief editor of the literary magazine.

BAD AND GOOD THINGS ABOUT DIVORCE

Brandon, age twelve:
Bad: You don't trust your parents anymore.
Good: When you ask for something,
you have a better chance of getting it.

Funny-Looking Feet

At some age all kids from divorced families probably hope they can get their parents to make up. They want them to reunite. When I was six, I remember thinking, "Mom and Dad are still married. They just don't live together."

But that was then, and this is now. I'm eighteen tomorrow. I've had twelve years' experience. From what I've seen, I feel that in a divorce, no matter what's going on between the parents, everyone does better if you—their child—aren't dragged into their fight.

And no matter whether you see both parents always or never, nothing changes the fact that they are the two individuals who came together to create you. Your smiles, your heart, even your funny-looking feet are what they are because of your two biological parents.

Divorce happens. You can make from it the worst possible life—or the best. The choice, in the end, is up to you.

Final Thoughts

Part Two ☀

For Parents

Introduction ☁

You're divorced. You feel guilty. You remarry. You feel guilty. You worry, have your actions turned your children into the walking wounded? Have their chances for a happy, secure future been derailed before they even got rolling?

That's the widely publicized belief. In fact, divorce and remarriage are accepted as today's magic bullet in reverse. They are one-stop shopping for the source of kids' problems. Your daughter acts out, belittles and rages at you? It's the divorce. It's the new marriage. Your son physically threatens you and spends his time with troubling friends? It's the divorce. It's the new marriage. In some ways it is easier to have a convenient catchall on which to attach blame.

What's ignored, though, is that in general these conclusions of preordained doom are based on skewed, narrowly defined, homogeneous populations: children already in therapy; children from one specific geographic region; children solely from a small sample of the middle class.

This book instead looks and listens to a cross section of more than a thousand preteens and teenagers. Some are in therapy. Most aren't. They are being raised in a diverse range of economic conditions and live everywhere from rural America to dense urban sprawl. They are every race, creed, and color.

The news that comes through from them is clear. That these youngsters' hearts are seared by divorce can't be denied. But neither can their survival skills. Children are wonderfully, thankfully, miraculously resilient. They adapt to the world around them. They can find their versions of happy endings. You, though, must lead.

EMOTIONAL MINEFIELD

Your ability to set the direction, along with your children's willingness to follow your lead, makes the difference in the size and duration of their life scars. If you—the parent—establish and maintain the role of adult; if you don't turn your kids into confidants, message bearers, or sounding boards; if you handle these changes as best you can, your sons and daughters have a jump start on successfully getting through these complications.

There are dangerous obstacles, which in turn mean you'll find no single route through this emotional minefield. Some days you feel you've moved one step forward and two steps back. An approach to achieve a degree of stability works for six months, then begins to fail. What's a hot spot Monday, isn't Tuesday as some new crisis takes shape on the horizon.

And all day, every day, any ongoing issue makes your job harder. A spouse's disappearance, a family member's alcoholism or drug addiction, a history of violence in the home, abuse or neglect of your children, financial upheaval, and so on, can overwhelm the best intentions.

Still, advice, counsel, and resources literally surround you. Look at your own life and those of your relatives, your friends, the members of your local and on-line communities. This book guides you in what might be available and what questions to ask. All these resources serve as reminders that you are not alone. You are on a communal journey to build a new life for yourself and your children.

SECRET JOURNALS

Part one of this book may have made you feel like you stumbled on your children's secret journals. Some preteens and teenagers wrote and talked about their confusion. Some drew their feelings or family portraits. Others let their anger roar. Still others took you along as they worked out resolutions. During this process their thoughts had a raw quality, as well as an honesty, power, and, yes, at times even a sweet, unintended humor.

Then they attempted to answer the questions that may haunt you, questions you do not yet know how to ask your own offspring: Do you feel the separation/divorce is your fault? Do you hope that we'll get back together? Do you understand why we divorced?

Providing a more detailed insight, seven preteens sat down for interviews. Afterward family therapists pinpointed the story told between the lines and discussed how you and your youngsters can best handle similar issues.

But the kid's-eye view predominated. They often seemed more willing to listen to one another than to parents whom they must relearn to trust. In this effort they also offered nuts-and-bolts advice on such typical problems as parents feuding, dividing holidays, and, if asked, deciding which parent to live with. In the last chapter two teens, themselves veterans of family divorce, acted as role models on achieving happy endings.

DIRECTION SIGNALS

For over a year I met not only kids leading lives dissected and reconnected by divorce and remarriage, I also talked to you and your peers. I started with those closest to my life and traveled out in concentric circles.

I interviewed divorce lawyers, a financial expert, a mediator, a communication skills specialist, a divorced Webmaster, a Banana Splits director, a judge, a rabbi, an imam, preachers, teachers, school counselors, librarians, therapists, psychologists, and youth workers.

From that list I picked a variety of representative sources, experts offering advice about getting you and your children grounded. They are not the only people with whom to talk. Instead they are meant to give you examples of what sort of help is available to you.

Now you can read what these experts have to say. Look

at the people's titles. Skim the chapter until you come to the person you'd most like to hear from. Begin there. See what problems and solutions resonate with what you're experiencing. Let them be your direction signals until you arrive at a clearer sense of which way to travel.

COMMON PROBLEMS

You and your children could first read this book alone and then make time to go through the most relevant parts together. By focusing on the lives of others with whom you have various issues in common, you have a neutral place to start your own conversations. And it will take far more than a single conversation.

Any transition is hard. Children feel most comfortable and secure with the familiar. You are changing all that. The future is uncharted. They feel out of balance. They feel buried under the weight of emotions that scare them. Often a person they love is leaving them. Their heart is broken and they don't understand what happened.

You are not at your most focused. You have to use enormous energy simply to keep yourself together. In that process you may not have the strength to give your children the attention, love, and care they need, especially during this time of crisis. Reach out and take advantage of the help around you. Share the burden.

And finally, a wish: May the voices on these pages join with yours and your sons' and daughters' to bring you all a renewed sense of peace.

☁ Chapter 7

A Divorced Mother's Perspective

Who is a "typical" divorced mother? Each person's story is special and unique, with many factors coming together to form it.

For example, many women suffer from increased money problems. With this woman—who separated when her daughter and son, Cali and Dennon, were six and nine—that wasn't the case. The purpose of this book is to get you started looking at the emotional, not the financial, fallout.

This mother's goal is to talk about how she tried to analyze what exactly went wrong with the separation and divorce, and how to find solutions.

I guess that most of you about to separate and divorce have no idea what you're getting into.

You're "insane." And when you're that way, you don't make the best decisions. Mainly you want out. The change, you think, will make everything better. In that state of mind you're supposed to sit down with this person you're leaving to discuss uncomfortable and painful issues, especially ones dealing with the kids, like custody.

PLAY MARRIED

I found that custody arrangements were a huge problem. If the other parent is a nut, it can be worse yet. For example, Matt, my ex-husband, was, among other things, a megalomaniac. It was hard to break up with him.

He kept insisting that we stay together. And why not? I took care of everything—most of the income, the house, the books, the doctor's appointment arrangements, the school meetings. Matt's specialty was to put the kids on his back or swing them around. He was good, though, with emergency health problems.

Anyway, I wanted to keep Cali and Dennon with me but not deny their father. Matt's solution was to "play married" for various events. Say the kids were coming home from camp. He'd show up on the doorstep, ready for dinner.

Or there was a school hockey game. I had a car. He didn't. Matt would call and say, "When are we going to the game?" He's physically large. He steals the moment. I'd feel back to being his parcel. I'd comment on all his put-downs.

Then I decided, Let it be. Don't say a word. I'd tell him, "Get there on your own." So he would, and he'd sit looking sad on the other side of the field. It was painful for the kids.

What happened, I wondered, to our talks about trying to be respectful of the moments with Cali and Dennon? What happened to the idea that their stability was important?

In a world of ideal parents, they would move and the kids would stay in the same house. In our imperfect world Matt and I divided the weeks, with equal time with each parent. We thought it was the fairest.

Dennon said to me, "Don't worry, Mom. I'm okay with it." Then I heard him calling a friend, saying, "Come over next week. My parents separated and Dad's moved to a building with a pool."

Cali, though, cried all the time. Finally she said to me, "It's so awful going back and forth. First I have to take care of you. Then Dad. And now you want me to take ceramics class! I can't do it."

Of course I felt guilty about what she said. But I didn't know what to do other than believe most adults flounder with this issue. The fine-tuning of custody teaches you that holidays will forever be hell. Whichever formula you come up with—do holidays together, split them, alternate years, have two Thanksgivings, and so on—nothing seems to work. With those who claim they have it down pat, I'm suspicious. Custody arrangements should at least give you some time off.

SWARMS OF COUSINS

When you divorce, in some ways you feel diminished. Literally, the family size is smaller. Early on in the separation I took the kids on vacation. I considered us a full family. Cali didn't. She was embarrassed. "Where's the daddy figure?" she kept saying.

I decided I had to encourage Cali and Dennon to see all their grandparents on a regular basis. It was no secret I didn't like Matt's parents. They were always annoying. Still, they were the grandparents of my kids. They can be generous of spirit. My mother-in-law made herself aggressively available.

I also reminded myself that my sister had three great kids. We started to do a lot together. There'd be this sweet swarm of cousins. The sheer number of family members interacting helped all the kids feel more secure in life. Or that's what I hoped.

A GOOD NEXT GUY

God wants a family with an adult in charge, not adolescent parents. At first sex and dating became a huge issue for me. I was breaking up my marriage because I was dissatisfied.

I thought, I'll get divorced. There'll be a good next guy. We'll get married and move on. I was wildly looking, hungry for the excitement of a romantic prospect. I was also self-conscious, lonesome, and felt I was living on failed dreams.

I had a variety of affairs.

Kids can be funny. Only after my relationships were over would they tell me what they thought. With the first guy Dennon said, "What a bum." He saw more and faster than I did. Finally I felt obligated to spend more time with them. And it was seductive. I like both my children so much, and the way they think.

Even though this whole experience has meant they've

grown up faster, I try not to burden them by sharing confidences. I try to let them lead. Lately I've been feeling I should do even more with them. But then I worry, Am I overinvesting in them, probably because of my guilt?

I try not to let Cali and Dennon see me when I'm upset. It only upsets them. Now the separation has changed into divorce. They know I'm not so much in outer space as I was when it started.

They know we're lucky compared to some of their friends. Money hasn't been a real problem. Matt sometimes made money, but he didn't always bring it home. When my mom died last year, I got a lump sum. He felt entitled to some of it.

I think my kids are wonderful. They're success stories in terms of falling apart, getting help, finding out who they are, and moving forward. I just wish people would understand that divorce can often turn out to be something healthy.

Yady, age thirteen:

DAD'S GOOD-NIGHT KISS

When the sun goes down
You wait for a kiss
But he's not around to hug and to twist.
You don't know why he's gone
But you wish he weren't far
So he could come along and give you that kiss.

The stars don't shine as bright,
But you know it's for the best, your
Mother's not hurt. Your brothers
Aren't crying, and the baby is asleep.
What else do you want? You still
Want that kiss?

You shouldn't cry longer
You should just be stronger
For you and your brothers
Who deserve peace and love.

Chapter 8

A Divorced Father's Perspective

For all the media attention child-raising single dads receive, their number still remains relatively small. They were also less willing to talk. And they don't turn to support groups, community organizations, and on-line resources as often as women do. However, this father—who separated when his daughters, Juliet and Sarah, were ten and twelve—was ready to share his thoughts, as long as he could first write them in E-mails to me. I edited those and sent back more questions, a process we repeated over a period of several months.

Neither this dad nor the single mom in chapter 7 has remarried. Since finishing these interviews, the man has fallen in love. Once more he's thinking about a walk down the aisle. Because remarriages have such complex and varied family entanglements, and consid-

ering space limitations, in part two you'll find only these less complicated stories.

I'm a successful businessman and lawyer. Often in my life I've managed to change the course of events through sheer force of will. One day, though, I realized that wouldn't be the case with my marriage to Sally. Although I was committed to the idea of my family, I wasn't getting a lot of my needs met. I sought solace elsewhere and began a destructive long-term affair. After I was found out, after I allowed myself to see my wife's grief and humiliation, I tried to mend my marriage. I thought I had done a good job, but the trust couldn't be rebuilt. Ultimately Sally decided she wanted out. Five years ago she told me she was filing for divorce.

We then had to deal with money and come up with an equitable settlement. I made a generous offer. Sally, however, went into a rage—as did her mother, who called my mother to tell her, among other things, that I was horrible.

In the past I'd managed the family assets, while also sitting on the boards of various entities. Now, according to my offer, in addition to alimony she'd have to deal with a range of business decisions, something she'd never done before. That scared her. I learned I had to remove my ego and see the issue from her point of view. Once I could do that, we worked out the details.

INTERVENTION

Four years ago Sarah, my older daughter, said she wanted to start staying with me. "Have you talked with your mom about this?" I asked her. When she told me she hadn't, I said that although the decision was her mother's, I'd bring it up. Sally agreed to this new arrangement.

A couple years later Juliet made the same choice. At that point in their lives they wanted stability and a certain parental influence. Their mother, they said, was doing the club scene and dating a twenty-three-year-old. They wanted an intervention to get her to be more like "Mom." Kids embarrass easily, and Mom was an embarrassment to them.

I tried just to listen to what they had to say, to stay uninvolved and make no judgments. I also decided to continue to pay Sally child support. I didn't have to, but I thought it'd reduce the chance of any of us getting upset. I was learning to take the larger, longer view, focusing on the impact on the girls, along with my own peace of mind.

A NEW FAMILY

Now time has passed. Because Sally doesn't want to lose contact with the girls, she picks up Juliet for school each day. On birthdays we go out to dinner together, just like the family of old. At Christmas we get gifts for them that say, FROM MOM AND DAD.

The two of us talk frequently about kid issues in order to ensure we're in sync. We work to make sure we think of our daughters first—and avoid competing for their love. Most importantly, we want them to know they are loved, and I think we've been able to do that.

During Thanksgiving I looked at the table before we sat down to eat and realized my daughters had made all the essentials for the marvelous classic dinner. Afterward they finished the evening with a game of Monopoly.

The three of us, I saw, had created a new family. We had new traditions and new memories. Together we'd gone to New York City and Hawaii. But I believe what we all value even more are the shared experiences of the most ordinary variety, just living our lives.

I remember thinking when I was Mr. Mom ironing Sarah's gown for graduation, I spent years getting home late, missing dinner, being unavailable, and being selfish. I feel now I have the opportunity to make up for lost time and develop an extraordinary relationship with my daughters.

Ivan, age sixteen:

TEARING ME APART

I was happy with my mom and dad.
Life was dandy with my sister.
Lived, like the American dream.
Lived like Americans.
Had a dog of my own.
Had a room of my own with Sega and Nintendo.
Lived like a king.
Had very caring family members.
We were very happy.

Mom did not like Dad anymore.
Dad did not like Mom.
My dog was gone.

My room was gone.
My sister was not dandy.
I had no more Sega and Nintendo.
I had no love anymore.
I only had Dad; Mom was gone.
My mom does not like me.
I was not loved anymore.
Why?
Divorce tore me apart from the American dream.

And my daughters are, by the way, very interested in whom I may date. They have strong opinions and do not hesitate to express them. They tell me whether they like the woman, and they even suggest I should date someone they know, such as the mother of a fellow student.

For about a year after Sally and I separated, I didn't get involved with anyone. Then I met a woman with whom I thought I might have a serious relationship. After some time passed I introduced her to Sarah and Juliet. They liked her and her daughter, who was younger. We all went to Disney World together. But by the end of a year the promise was gone and the relationship over.

Since then I've not been involved to the point where I felt it was appropriate to invite a woman into our life in that way. I make a point of not having women to the house and introducing them to the girls if they are just casual dates. No one has spent the night.

I sometimes wonder, Am I waiting for Juliet to graduate from high school before I make that transition to even think of marriage again?

I feel that the key to a woman's successful relationship with a man resides in the nature of her relationship with her father. I try to be a supportive father and encourage my daughters to understand they are only limited by their imaginations.

Sarah is not interested in college. She is a ballet dancer and hopes to pursue that career. Juliet says she wants to get a college basketball scholarship, to be an actress, and to be the president of the United States. "I trust you implicitly," I tell them both. "You don't have to earn it."

If I were to give advice to parents going through divorce, I'd tell them, "Put your children first. Create a positive and stable environment for them, one they can count on. And don't involve your kids in the internecine conflicts with your former spouse. Do whatever it takes to get past your own anger and fear."

CD Chapter 9

Teachers', Librarians', and Youth Workers' Advice

During their day, your children come in contact with a potential array of adults. These teachers, librarians, and youth workers see kids from different perspectives. In this chapter these experts speak to the issue of divorce and remarriage, what they observe of its fallout, and what you might do to ease the transition.

The following answers were selected from those given by thirty-five teachers in a class at Saginaw Valley State University, Saginaw, Michigan; fifty media specialists at a meeting at the Donnell Center of the New York Public Library; twenty-five media specialists at a meeting at the Bellevue Public Library, Bellevue, Washington; and one hundred *members of the Utah Corrections Association at a state conference in St. George, Utah. Their words come from the heart but are grounded in both personal and professional experience.*

Preschool teacher:

Both parents still need to be involved with school life. Even if you don't feel comfortable with each other, think how your children will feel if you don't show up for important activities.

Kindergarten teacher:

You should tell teachers about any life-changing events that affect your children in the classroom.

Elementary school teacher:

Everyone needs the reassurance of having a home. Many kids talk about "Mom's house" and "Dad's house," never "my house" or "our house." You need to work hard to make your children know it's their home, too.

Elementary school teacher:

Make life as predictable as possible. Kids should know ahead of time where they'll be from night to night. Too much uncertainty causes their mind to wander.

Elementary school teacher:

Children who've had several "dads" in the home by the time they are seven or eight seem mistrustful and distant.

Children act out more when they are put in the middle between Mom and Dad. In my experience they cope better all around when they have a strong sense that both parents still love them.

Middle school teacher:

Yes, your kids need you, but also remind them that parents are human. You may say or do things that you later regret. They should try to forgive you, share their feelings, and learn from your mistakes.

Middle school teacher:

Make time to listen to your kids, to talk to them, or just to go for a walk together. When you respond with your eyes, ears, heart, and soul, children sense it. They heal and grow.

Music teacher:

I hurt for students in split families where the single parent won't allow participation in choir, band, or orchestra. Often it's because of tight scheduling and lack of transportation. But music can bring an inner peace. It shouldn't be dismissed as unimportant. I'm a divorced mom, too, with a twelve-year-old daughter. She is my light—and my music.

Social worker:

Children most often live up to the expectations you put on them, whether positive or negative. Even if you're going through a personally terrible time, press your kids to be good, optimistic, and achieving. Without that adult guidance, they are more likely to fail.

Youth corrections officer:

Try to have an adult in the home when the kids come home from school. Have activities for them after homework is finished. It could be something as simple as playing catch, building a model rocket, or listening to them practice piano. Children have to know they are more than just people you have to take care of.

Corrections administrator:

Youngsters involved in sports programs, scouting, and other community activities use these programs as their release for emotional pain. It also helps them keep from getting into trouble during troubling times.

Media specialist:

Surround yourself with people who are positive and supportive. No naysayers are needed. If you're not the one who wants the divorce, the period of mourning will be more difficult. Reach out for help. Once you can focus again, do things that will be exciting to you. This will make you a better parent to your children.

Media specialist:

I was twelve when my parents divorced. There was a lot of venom between them, and it colored my whole adolescence. Kids need someone of their own—not a parent—to be on their side.

Media specialist:

The negative allusions to single-parent families are tiresome. I see lots of kids doing well despite any losses due to divorce.

Chapter 10 ☁️

Many children talk about the benefit of Banana Splits and similar school-based programs where trained adults help them deal with divorce and remarriage. Not all parents know schools provide such a service. Before you suggest to your youngsters that they participate, here are some details.

Valerie Raymond, Ph.D.
Psychologist and Banana Splits Coordinator
Friends Seminary
New York, New York

With divorce lots of kids feel they're the only one in this pickle. Often, too, they think they caused it. To help children cope, increasing numbers of schools offer discussion groups called Banana Splits.

These groups are free, voluntary, and take place within the school day. At our school we meet during lunch for thirty minutes about twice a month. We've found students tend to stay three to four years—from the immediate shock at the news through a mourning period, their parents dating, and even remarriage.

While Banana Splits is not seen as a therapy situation, kids are instructed in the basic of confidentiality. They come in and tell their story. They leave and tell their story. They don't tell other people's stories.

LIVING WITH LOSS

In an open spot in the school we display a membership tree. Students can check it out. Then if there's a split in the family, with parental approval they can cut out a banana, write their name on it, and hang it on the tree. The fact that there is a large community of children in this situation becomes clear. It's a daily reminder they're not alone.

In the room where we meet there's a long piece of butcher paper. Before we start talking, or during the discussion, kids can get up and write their thoughts without signing their name. Then by scanning what's up there, the leader—or leaders—can discuss that topic. Because serious issues like health, violence, and substance abuse often figure within a split family, the group allows these topics to be talked about. But the focus is mainly on living with the loss.

Parents' dating is a hotly debated topic, as is remarriage. For those children who don't see a parent, usually the dad, the need to understand why he doesn't get in touch, that yearning, is just palpable. The problem of a parent asking a child to keep things secret, or the reverse, asking a child to tell the other parent something, also troubles kids.

The leader asks, "Who's been through this?" and kids begin explaining their suggestions and strategies on how to deal with the issue at hand. Afterward the adults running the program add their piece.

Children are encouraged to go home and talk to parents about the topics that come up. And a number of times a year parents are encouraged to come in or meet on their own. Also, parents can contact the leaders anytime. Of course the school is involved, too. The administration and teachers have to be fully supportive of Banana Splits.

At the end of each school year we have a picnic. To build a sense of continuity, the alumni are always invited. Kids who've aged out and feel they no longer need Banana Splits still return for this special occasion.

Oscar, age ten:

GO AWAY

Please don't stay
The fights
The confusion
The child neglect
It is too much stress
The family is broken
The bills aren't paid
There is sadness
So please
Go away!

Chapter 11

Communication Skills Specialist's Advice

Children often don't want to hear parents' speeches, starting with the one about their separation. A student-created "no ears" drawing (see page 71) is a graphic reminder—he is tuning them out. However, these major life changes require a series of ongoing conversations with children. Judy Pollock takes her background as a teacher, blends it with her work in theater, and adds her talents as a respected expert in communication skills.

Her "practice" sessions were spent with her own two children, discussing life during her and their father's separation and divorce.

Judy Pollock
Communication Skills Specialist
President, Language at Work, Inc.
Washington, D.C.

Any conversation with your kids can feel like you're heading into a minefield. When the topic is divorce, it's hard to avoid explosions. Still, there are basic ways to present information that can make emotionally dangerous conversations less threatening all around.

1. **Think about your audience, in this case your children. How much do they need to know and what are their issues?**
2. **Decide on the main purpose of the conversation, for example, breaking the news about the divorce.**
3. **Organize your thoughts—how and what exactly do you want to tell them?**
4. **Deliver the information.**
5. **Come to closure.**

Easy, right? Not at first.

The difficulty is that most people begin at step four. You focus on this single delivery, and you want to get to the point immediately. "People change. Your mom/dad and I no longer agree. We're getting a divorce," you tell your children, forgetting that these kinds of topics take more than a single conversation.

Now you're halfway through your speech, wondering, Where do I go from here? and your kids are busily filling in the blanks. Oh, my gosh, they think, if I change, will I be out the door?

Before you even start this discussion, go back to steps one, two, and three, reminding yourself who you're talking to, their ages, what they want and need, and that it's best to be specific.

KIDS' AGENDA

In sales, before talking about what you have to offer, you find out what's on the customer's mind. Up front you ask, "Tell me about your concerns," followed by, "So you're saying this is how you feel about this issue?"

The same approach can work with your children. Picture this conversation:

Parent: *"Maybe the divorce is not news to you. Did you suspect something was happening?"*

Kids: *"Yeah, you two have been screaming at each other all the time. We didn't even want to bring friends over. We never knew what might be going on."*

You've now learned two things to talk about that might not have been on your agenda: The fights bothered them; they were afraid to have their friends in your home. You could discover, too, that what children want to know may not have much to do with what you're telling them.

Parent: *"Mom and Dad love you very much. Everything will be the same."*

Kids think: *That's not what happened with our friends.*

Kids say: *"Will we have to move the way Jeremy did? What did we do wrong to make this happen?"*

They might even ask, "Why are you and Daddy/ Mommy getting divorced?" You know your children best. You want them to trust you. You have to decide how to present certain information in a neutral way.

Beyond that, however, let's say one of you adults, Mom or Dad, has nearly spent the family into bankruptcy, topped off by building a deck on the house. You may hate that soon-to-be ex-spouse, but you don't want to assign blame.

In kid language make the response about you, not your spouse. You could say, "There were some behaviors I couldn't accept. Dad/Mom and I have different opinions on how to spend our family money."

You could also add a statement such as this: "I have a lot of anger toward your father/mother, and I have a hard time talking about it." It's okay for kids to hear that you're angry. Then if you do lose your temper, you can tell them why in a context they understand. Remember, too, your kids will probably talk to their other parent. That person will balance what you say. If you are clear and straight with them, you'll feel better. And you won't get in trouble later.

ART OF LISTENING

How do you find out what your children want to hear? Listen to them. Listening is an active art, where for a while you're not talking and you indicate to the speakers that what they're saying has your approval. Often adults give kids the message that you're listening as long as they're saying what you want to hear.

For some of these conversations you might want to

exhibit vulnerability yourself. Here's a possible opening:

Parent: "Thinking about divorce is a little scary. It makes me nervous. Do you feel that way?"

If the answer is yes, you can then, among other things, move on to specific situations that might be frightening to them—a change of school, home, or friends. Of course, your children might say:

Kids: "No, we're not nervous . . . worried . . . scared."

Don't be discouraged by this type of answer. How they respond often has to do with what your relationship has been up to now. These conversations may be a new way of communicating and cover things you've never discussed before.

If they have trouble expressing what's going on inside their heart, try to think of names for feelings that aren't so upsetting. If they can't seem to say, "I'm really sad," together come up with sentences like "I'm confused" or "Sometimes I don't know why I feel blue." Then end that conversation with the reminder that they can always ask you to help sort out their feelings. If this helps, good. But even if they're still resistant to opening up, they've learned those funny feelings have a name, they are real, and Dad or Mom has them, too.

You can also ask them directly what they want to know. Some children aren't sure they have the right to know such things as "Why did you yell at Dad/Mom about drinking?" You have to guide them. They're already feeling pressure. They don't need additional stress, such as:

Parent: "Now that your dad/mom and I have separated, I'm going to expect you to be the big boy/little mother. You have to be a good example for your younger siblings."

Kid thinks: What does that mean!¿

Think about the questions you ask and the statements you make. Keep it simple. Just say, "I hope you'll help me with your little brother and sister." That lets your kids know you are in this together.

You also want to let them know that you'll talk about all this again. And again. In fact, whenever it's on their mind, they can come to you and talk some more. You don't want to leave them in the dark.

There may be times when you realize you haven't focused many conversations on what's happening. It's too painful. This is an opportunity to say, "I feel we haven't talked much about this. I know it's been hard. If you'd like, we could just sit here and think about our feelings." Then give them a hug and tell them how much you love them.

Chapter 12

Pastor's Advice

Some look for a commonsense solution to divorce and remarriage problems. Others turn to God. I spoke with ministers, priests, rabbis, imams, and so on. The Reverend Tom Wise, among others, tried to look at the issues in an honest, direct, and modern way. If what he says strikes a chord with you, you could turn to your local place of worship and see what counseling services it offers.

The Reverend Tom Wise
Pastor, Open Door Christian Church
Petaluma, California

I have to say this: If there's any way to make your marriage work, do it. The pain and consequence of divorce are far bigger than you imagine.

You probably see divorce as a solution to your problems. In reality, though, it may create more. Get help. Invest in marriage counseling. Even if you have to borrow the money, it's cheaper than a divorce.

At our church we don't charge for counseling. Check in your community, at your church or synagogue, to see what's available. If during the counseling you work things out, it's the best investment you could make.

HEAL AND RESOLVE

Even if you've already separated, I have you come to the church and we talk together for a half hour. During the first of several meetings we get a picture of what your marriage is like. It's painful to look for the wounds and destructive patterns of behavior. Plus, some couples can't be together without fierce anger toward each other. To deal with that I ask for permission to call "Stop" if the conversation gets too heated.

Often we discover that your marriage has good qualities gone awry. I remember a husband and wife who loved each other, but she said he never listened to her—to hear her heart. He's a problem solver. She'd start to communicate, and he'd jump in with an instant solution.

In one sense that was laudable. He was good at it. But it hurt her. Finally I helped them put together a structure where if she needed to talk to him, she would tell him to listen for a few minutes without interrupting.

Others need help in such basics as making time for just you two alone. We establish that as a goal, and then each week I ask, "Did you find a few hours for yourself as a couple? If not, why?"

I try, too, to give people guidelines. "You have to be careful with friends of the opposite sex," I might say. "It's better if they're friends with you and your mate, and your visiting is as a couple." You see, obviously, adultery takes enormous forgiveness. Not all affairs are addictive behavior. Often people never intend to end up in affairs. They were unguarded, shared too much with someone at work, went through a difficult time.

Some marriages aren't healable. Others are. But I still prepare those who have strayed. There are going to be times when pain and hate overcome your spouse. However, part of the good word of God is that he is forgiving. Maybe your spouse can resolve to forgive you.

Families come in different sizes and shapes. Octavia's uncle, her mother's brother, has lived with them for the last three years. This is fine with Octavia, as long as he keeps his boom box.

GOOD FORGIVERS

How you explain your separation and divorce to your children in the context of a God-centered life depends, I think, on what picture you've been painting for your kids of your faith. Maybe you've taught them that having a life of faith does not mean you're perfect. And being a good Christian means recognizing that everyone has problems. You're trying to be honest in your feelings, and you're asking God for help.

You might also want to say to your children, "Would you please forgive Mom and Dad for the problems that we have? For the weaknesses we have? For the pain we've brought you?" Children are good forgivers. Give them this chance.

FAITHFUL COMMITMENTS

After you split up, you've got to be faithful to the commitments you make to your children. To all parents who leave I say, "You have got to call your children. You have got to go over." Think about what you say. They don't need to be wowed and won over with trips to Disneyland. Do something simple with them, what you used to do together. Take them to school. Go for a walk to the park. Take along their best friends.

Add the issue of dating to all those life and financial changes. My best advice is to delay as long as possible. Even when you put it off, it's still likely your children will hate that person. Keep your dating discreet and apart from kids. They're in shock. They're hoping Mom and Dad will get back together. Often their great fantasy is to be the ones to reunite you.

More than once you should say to your children, "You had nothing to do with the divorce. Your mom/dad and I just haven't been able to work out our problems in a way to allow our marriage to continue. You can divorce a mate and he or she is no longer your mate, but your children are always your children."

Then hug them, saying again, "I love you."

OLD-COUNTRY PASTOR

I recommend premarital counseling, even if it's not the first time around. Even if it's the old-country pastor who only meets once with you. Statistics prove that this counseling has a large and measurable effect on decreasing the divorce rate.

Chapter 13 ☁

Most religious institutions now provide some type of counseling. Of those I came across while researching divorce and remarriage, Moving On, a program sponsored by a southern California Jewish Family Service office, served as a solid example. It can also serve as a model to use in describing what you are looking for in your community. Barbara Lanzet brought to the task her enthusiasm, developmental knowledge, personal experience, and a caring perspective.

Barbara Lanzet, L.C.S.W., B.C.D.
Supervisor, Special Projects–Moving On
Jewish Family Service
San Fernando Valley Adult and Children's Services
West Hills, California

For even the most resilient family, transition times are tough. During separation, divorce, or remarriage you need to create a new structure from what you've been together in the past to what you will be in the future.

Our purpose is to remind you that your family's not broken; it's restructuring. And you're not alone in the process.

At our meetings the adults and kids initially go into different rooms. You cover the same issues, but they're geared to your perspective. For instance, the first night both groups discuss family identity. The children then rejoin their parents, stepparents, or any significant others and are asked to draw the members in the form of a family shield.

It's interesting to see who ends up in the picture—from the dad they haven't seen in six months to the abusive relative who's still important in the child's eyes. Afterward we talk about all of that.

HOME BASE

At meetings we educate parents about what's developmentally appropriate, so in a sense they know what to expect. Even though every case has to be considered individually, we believe a child, especially a small one, needs a home base. Developmentally, passing toddlers around is not good for them. A two-year-old is in the separation anxiety stage. Most children that age do better with a primary caretaker, although they definitely need contact with the other parent.

At age four many children want to spend time with the opposite-sex parent. Little girls want to be with Daddy; little boys want to be with Mom. At about age six it turns around. Girls say, "I want to go shopping with Mommy."

Once you are familiar with this type of information, you're less likely to take it personally and feel hurt. You need to know, too, that no matter what the children do, no matter which of you they're with, they feel guilt.

By the time they're eight to twelve years old, while they're struggling for some autonomy, they still need to do things with the parent. You should learn tasks together, be involved in Boy Scouts and Girl Scouts, soccer, and hockey—or at least schlepp them from one activity to another.

FINE-TUNING RELATIONSHIPS

Nearly all children resent any life change. And they've already had a big change with the separation and/or divorce. If you date right away, it can frighten them. Are they supposed to attach to this new person? Is this person a replacement for Mom or Dad? What if she or he also vanishes? It's your job to keep the family boundaries and not burden your kids more. This theory, of course, is easier to discuss than to keep in effect.

You're under stress. You need time to fine-tune your family relationships. Your kids seem angry with you. You decide, I'll change my plans, stay home, and have a little quality time together. What happens? Your kids are indeed angry, want absolutely nothing to do with you, and you are sitting alone, fuming, wondering why you reworked things in the first place.

During the part of the evening when adults and children come back together, we look for ways to turn these kinds of scenarios into positive experiences.

Our meetings are held at Jewish Family Service. We always have interfaith marriages in the group. We talk about Jewish rituals and observances, as well as those of other religions. We also discuss the problems and delights of learning about different cultures and beliefs.

What if you agreed, for example, that your kids should be brought up in a specific religion, and that's the one of your almost ex-spouse? What if your children have always gone to your mother-in-law's for Passover? You know she'll feel the emptiness of not having them at the table. What if the other grandparents don't want to wake up Christmas morning without their grandchildren under their roof?

Together as a group we try to work out the problems of double heritages. Getting a divorce, we hear from you, doesn't change your relationship with God. And you never divorce your children.

For many reasons divorce is sad. But it's not a total loss. Unexpected, supportive, and exciting worlds can open to you and your offspring. The final goal of Moving On is to help all family members feel that and to help lift your heart's burden.

Help is available all around. It's up to you to reach out for the right mix. You can try all or none of the types of people suggested in this book. Their best collective opinion, however, is you can't navigate a divorce and remarriage alone. It's too tough and stressful.

Some of you might find comfort, knowledge, and power in therapy. I talked to therapists, school counselors, psychologists, and psychiatrists. Therapist Andrea Osnow specializes in the interactions of families. She agreed to take the extra time, meet individually and in a group setting, and answer all my questions.

Finding the best therapist is a highly personal matter. For that, you're on your own.

Andrea Osnow,[*] A.C.S.W.

Family Therapist

New York, New York

I'm a therapist. Many of my adult clients are children of divorce repeating the core issues. I hear, "When I was a kid, there was no one to talk to about these problems." Now they discover they can't form long-lasting relationships or they have a lot of conflict with their partner. They also have unresolved difficulties with their parents.

"You can come to therapy," I say, "and have me tell you, 'Yes, this is what happened to you.' You can continue not to deal with it or you can make choices and live your life differently. But if you don't deal with these issues, they'll get in the way."

I coach them to use the tool of letter writing to start the process. If possible, they go back in person to their family of origin to heal the wounds from their childhood. They want to ask their parents, for example, to talk about their divorce. What was it like? What were the problems for them? What about telling them and their siblings? Dealing with co-parenting? Money?

These conversations are especially important when there were such issues as abuse, neglect, or alcoholism. They contact family members and relatives to determine what exactly occurred and why no one stepped in. What should come out of these conversations is resolution and the ability to move ahead into a healthy relationship.

[*]For more information from Osnow and two other family therapists, Clio Garland and Ann Jackler, turn to part one, chapter 3.

150

They want to learn to trust, to negotiate, and to allow themselves to be close to someone.

BEFORE THE DIVORCE

I get people in here, mainly women, who just want out of the marriage. I say, "Are you prepared for this change? What are your skills? Do you need some training in a specific area? Remember, alimony is not enough. Also, once in the hands of a lawyer, the sweetest, most well-intentioned ex-partner can make your life awful."

Before the divorce you need to take responsibility for your future finances. Beyond child support you should find out such details as: What about the house? If you get it, can you afford to maintain it? Is there a pension plan? Will you still get part of it? What about taxes and the choices you make?

I try two things. I try to get you to see a divorce mediator instead of a lawyer. And I remind you that the poverty of women in divorce is an ongoing battle.

The parent, usually the father, who's been earning more of the family income shouldn't use money as a weapon. At a minimum you need to be responsible for your children's food and shelter. Some dads fight that, as well as potentially further limit the children's future. I'll always remember one dad who insisted, "I'll only pay part of college tuition, and only to a local community college." His kids are brilliant and could well get into the best schools.

Shaundra, age eleven:

Shaundra, her mother, and her brother live with her grandparents. Her father doesn't come around anymore.

CO-PARENTING AND
DEAD GUINEA PIGS

The phenomenon of joint custody—co-parenting—places a tremendous pressure and responsibility on kids. As parents, you need to accept that each of you has a different parenting style. Each household needs to be comfortable for your children, too. They're adaptable. If you're comfortable with what you've created for them, they are.

Children should be kept out of parental conflict. You shouldn't make them the bearer of messages: "You didn't pay Mom this month." And you shouldn't let your negative feelings about your ex-spouse be put on them. You should work to get to where the co-parenting relationship is calm enough that you can both go to school events, family weddings, and so on, without incredible tension.

Even in co-parenting, the mothers most often are the psychological parent. They're the ones aware the child needs a haircut. They buy the new toothbrush. They make the doctor's appointment. The fathers may want to share this role. But they've never been involved, and now they're suddenly trying to set up play dates, send cookies to school, be part of a car pool.

The other parents may not know the father as well. They may feel insecure having their children go to his home. Fathers may have to spend time getting to know their children's friends' families better. They may also find themselves tending the guinea pigs their children keep with them. They shouldn't be like the father I met with who went away on a business trip and returned to dead rodents.

HOT SPOTS

Here are a few hot spots in your future that you should be aware of—and a few words of advice.

1. **Extended Families: Whole families get divorced. It's up to parents to be mature enough to keep the kids' relationships going with the grandparents, cousins, and so on. And don't forget the in-laws. They don't know what to do, even if they have been close to your children. Show them the way. If you don't, the kids lose out.**

2. **Dating: You need to keep your dates separate from your**

children. Yes, often you want to talk about these new people in your life or you want to introduce them to your children. But my best advice is that unless it becomes serious, don't tell them many details. And you sure don't need to bring them home to spend the night. When your children start dating and you're dating, there's a kind of competition that can develop, particularly between mothers and daughters. With sons there's pressure to be the "man of the family." Those are all stereotypes, but they do happen.

3. **Remarried Families:** There is a whole category of moms who are left and feel envy when the former spouse remarries. You must work to deal with any jealousy you experience. When parents remarry, it is still your job to show discipline and work out those emotional issues with the co-parent.

   The stepparent's job is to be a friend. You should be clear with your children that the stepparent is not coming in and taking over, and that stepsiblings aren't loved more than they are. Privacy issues are also tricky. It's one thing to have a dad walk into children's rooms when they're in their undies. It's another thing to have a step-dad walk in. When the blended families are young enough to start a new family, you can't expect your children to be as excited as you are. New babies add a range of complicated issues to their life.

4. **Adolescence:** As your children start approaching adolescence, say twelve to thirteen, their needs begin to shift. For instance, they need to be able to have friends over to both households. You have to be flexible with these new

needs. Around fourteen or fifteen it's not unusual for kids to want to live with the other primary parent. The teen years in particular are vulnerable to the ramifications of divorce.

GENTLE AND REASSURING

My daughter, Carly, was seven when three of her friends went off to summer camp and came back to their parents divorcing. Two of the girls became moody. I told her, "When there's fighting and stress in a home, it can be upsetting to the family members. Maybe that's what's happening."

Then one night her father and I were arguing. Carly said, "Stop fighting or you'll get a divorce."

I tried to explain: "There are times when people disagree, just like when you and your brother get frustrated and yell at each other. It doesn't mean you don't still love each other. And it doesn't even mean there's going to be a winner and a loser."

She worried. Divorce was all around her. But that explanation was all right with her.

As you look to your future you and your children will have these kinds of conversations. Together you'll learn both the tough lessons of divorce and remarriage, along with the gentle and reassuring ones.

PRINT RESOURCES

Bolick, Nancy O'Keefe. *How to Survive Your Parents' Divorce.* New York: Franklin Watts, 1994. [Young Adult]

Braver, Sanford L., with Diane O'Connell. *Divorced Dads: Shattering the Myths.* New York: Jeremy P. Tarcher/Putnam, 1998. [Adult]

Bray, John, and John Kelly. *Stepfamilies: Love, Marriage, and Parenting in the First Decade.* New York: Broadway Books, 1998. [Adult]

Cane, Michael Allan. *The Five-Minute Lawyer's Guide to Divorce.* New York: Dell, 1995. [Adult]

Covey, Stephen R. *The 7 Habits of Highly Effective Families.* New York: Golden Books, 1997. [Adult]

Fisher, Helen E. *Anatomy of Love: A Natural History of Mating, Marriage, and Why We Stray.* New York: Fawcett Columbine, 1992. [Adult]

Gardner, Richard A. *Las preguntas de los niños sobre el divorcio.* Mexico: Trillas, 1995. [Young Adult]

Johnson, Linda Carlson. *Everything You Need to Know about Your Parents' Divorce.* New York: Rosen Publishing Group, 1992. [Young Adult]

———— *Todo lo que necesitas saber cuando tus padres se divorcian.* Mexico: Promexa, 1994. [Young Adult]

Kaganoff, Penny, and Susan Spano, eds. *Women on Divorce: A Bedside Companion.* New York: Harcourt Brace, 1995. [Adult]

Levine, Beth. Divorce: *Young People Caught in the Middle.* Springfield, N.J.: Enslow Publishing, 1995. [Young Adult]

Naylor, Sharon. *The Unofficial Guide to Divorce.* New York: Macmillan General Reference, 1998. [Adult]

Neuman, M. Gary, with Patricia Romanowski. *Helping Your Kids Cope with Divorce the Sandcastles Way.* New York: Times Books, 1998. [Adult]

Peck, Richard. *Unfinished Portrait of Jessica.* New York: Laurel Leaf, 1993. [Young Adult]

Wolf, Anthony E. *Why Did You Have to Get a Divorce? And When Can I Get a Hamster?* New York: Noonday Press, 1998. [Adult]

You can go to countless Web sites for help and information. However, today's best sites might not be the best ones when you're reading this book. When people think of the Web search component, often they have the impulse to go to one or two search engines, type in *divorce homepage,* and—get a lot of junk. Instead try lots of engines, such as Yahoo!, Infoseek, Excite, and so on, and type in additional search terms, including *family, pictures, visit, love,* and *kids.* That will give you a better selection.

In addition to the Web sites listed below, many kids have created their own homepages where parents can visit regularly; help with homework; work out details for upcoming holidays, overnights, appointments, etc.; and just stay connected. E-mail can work magic to help parents and children feel as if they are in continuous touch.

BBC Education: Children of Divorce
Homepage: **www.bbc.co.uk/education/divorce**

Children of Divorce is designed to help parents and children who may be dealing with a divorce. For example, as a starting point kids can follow the link "How to Cope When Your Parents Split Up" for answers even to the questions you might want to ask but haven't been able to.

Center for Divorce Education

Homepage: **www.divorce-education.com**

This is a nonprofit organization dedicated to teaching parents how to keep their children out of divorce-related conflicts.

Children of Separation and Divorce Center

Homepage: **cosd.bayside.net**

The Children of Separation and Divorce Center (COSD) is a private, nonprofit organization that offers, among other things, professional and peer counseling services, as well as community outreach and prevention programs. COSD staff have published a handbook for parents, *Talking to Your Children about Separation and Divorce,* and a document, "Guidelines for Child-Focused Decision Making."

Children's Rights Council

Homepage: **www.vix.com/crc**

The Children's Rights Council (CRC) is a national non-profit organization based in Washington, D.C., that works to assure children meaningful and continuing contact with both their parents and extended family, regardless of the parents' marital status. CRC has chapters in most of the United States.

Depression in Children

Homepage: **www.divorceinfo.com/depressioninchildren.htm**

This site describes depression in children of divorce, as well as the symptoms and what divorcing parents can do to deal with their kids when they're clinically depressed.

The Divorce Center

Homepage: **www.divorcenter.org**

The Divorce Center offers emotional and legal support for those dealing with separation, divorce, single parenting, and family issues.

Divorce: How It Affects Children

Homepage: **queendom.com/wwwboard/messages/234.html**

This is a bulletin board–type discussion site.

Divorce Magazine

Homepage: **www.divorcemag.com**

Published quarterly, *Divorce* contains articles on issues such as finances, custody and visitation, dating, and blended families.

DivorceNet: Family Law Advice

Homepage: **www.divorcenet.com**

This site has bulletin boards, chat rooms, FAQs, and articles on divorce, child support, custody, visitation, and more.

Divorce Source

Homepage: **www.divorcesource.com**

This site provides information pertaining to child custody, child support, alimony, counseling, visitation, individual rights, taxes, the legal process, and more.

The Divorce Support Page

Homepage: **www.divorcesupport.com**

This is a support site for people struggling with divorce,

dissolution, separation, custody, alimony, visitation, etc., and includes information about divorce professionals in your area who can help.

The Father Project

Homepage: **www.fatherproject.com**

The Father Project is a nonprofit organization that gives direction to fathers, mothers, and children seeking to heal the pains of family separation.

Parenting Q&A

Homepage: **www.parenting-qa.com/**

This is a question-and-answer site to help parents in particular minimize the impact of such issues as custody, mediation, separation, support, and visitation.

The Sandcastles Program

Homepage: **www.sandcastlesprogram.com/**

The Sandcastles Program is a group experience designed to assist children in dealing with their reaction to their parents' separation and/or divorce.

Solo: A Guide for the Single Parent

Homepage: **www.soloparenting.com**

Published quarterly, this magazine covers issues that single parents and their children are dealing with today.

For Better, For Worse is Janet Bode's fifteenth new title for young adults. Her unique approach—to offer story-based problem solving on today's issues—has generated both awards from organizations such as the American Library Association and fan mail from readers across the country. The advice she collected speaks so clearly to them they feel compelled to write. They have learned that ultimately these are books of hope and inspiration.

A frequent speaker in schools, libraries, at conferences, and on radio and television shows, including *The Oprah Winfrey Show, 20/20,* and *Larry King Live,* Bode lived in New York City. She died in December 1999.

Reporter/cartoonist Stan Mack has created weekly cartoon columns for the *Village Voice* and *Adweek* magazine, as well as occasional columns for such publications as the *New York Times, Natural History Magazine,* and *Print.* He has written and illustrated more than fifteen children's books. His latest book-length titles are *Stan Mack's Real Life American Revolution* and *The Story of the Jews: A 4,000 Year Adventure.* His current work in progress looks at parenting today. This is Bode and Mack's sixth collaboration.